"Clea!"

That voice. She jerked around like a puppet on a string, eyes stretched wide, shock punching the air out of her lungs.

Breathless, she whispered, "Brand...?"

It couldn't be. Disbelief made her blink. *Brand was dead.*

The man coming toward her was tall, dark and very much alive.

The hands that came down on her shoulders were so intimately familiar...yet so painfully strange. *He was dead.* Yet the fingers cupping her shoulders were warm, strong and very much alive.

This was no ghost.

This was a human. A man she knew too well.

Her husband was back.

* * *

To find out more about Desire's upcoming books and to chat with authors and editors, become a fan of Harlequin Desire on Facebook, www.facebook.com/HarlequinDesire, or follow us on Twitter, www.twitter.com/desireeditors!

Dear Reader,

Every now and then I get an idea that just won't leave me alone. The characters come to life—I can hear them talking. And this was one of those ideas.

In fact, the opening scene of *Reclaiming His Pregnant Widow* was so vivid in my mind, it took up permanent residence. A hero who was presumed dead comes back to town to find the woman he loves has had him declared dead. How would he respond? And what about his woman, who can't bear to think that her trust has been misplaced? I knew from the first moment that these characters would be in for a rocky ride.

When I discussed the idea with my first editor, Melissa Jeglinski, she loved it. But I wasn't ready to write the story…yet. I still had too many unanswered questions. My next editor, Krista Stroever, also believed in the idea—but both of us still had questions. Finally Charles Griemsman came along and the story came to life.

So I'm truly thrilled you'll at last have a chance to meet Brand and Clea after all the time that they've been living in my head!

Happy reading.

Tessa Radley

TESSA RADLEY

RECLAIMING HIS PREGNANT WIDOW

Recycling programs
for this product may
not exist in your area.

ISBN-13: 978-0-373-73135-0

RECLAIMING HIS PREGNANT WIDOW

TESSA RADLEY

loves traveling, reading and watching the world around her. As a teen Tessa wanted to be an intrepid foreign correspondent. But after completing a bachelor of arts degree and marrying her sweetheart, she became fascinated by law and ended up studying further and practicing as an attorney in a city firm.

A six-month break spent traveling through Australia with her family rewoke the yen to write. And life as a writer suits her perfectly—traveling and reading count as research, and as for analyzing the world…well, she can think "what if?" all day long. When she's not reading, traveling or thinking about writing, she's spending time with her husband, her two sons or her zany and wonderful friends. You can contact Tessa through her website, www.tessaradley.com.

For Charles

All my life November has been special.
It's my birthday month. It's Prince Charming month.
It's the best month ever!

So I'm dedicating this book to Charles
with gratitude and affection—
Charles, you will forever make me feel like Cinderella.
And meeting you was a hundred birthdays
wrapped into one. A magic, never-to-be-forgotten moment.

Thank you for your patience, for your grace
and your wonderful work.

One

The photograph sealed it.

The newspaper Brand Noble had bought at JFK International Airport on his return to the United States had carried a story about tonight's black-tie museum exhibition opening. But it was the photo of Clea standing beside a statue of a stone tiger that had caused his heart to stop. It had been four years since he'd seen his wife, and she looked more beautiful than ever. Her raven hair unchanged, her eyes still wide and green.

Brand was not about to allow anything as insignificant as the lack of an embossed invitation to keep him from her. He'd waited long enough.

Now, two hours later, Brand slammed the door of the yellow-and-black cab that had ferried him to Manhattan's Museum Mile. Turning his back on the midweek bustle of commuters hastening home in the fading light, he focused on the Museum of Ancient Antiquities towering ahead.

Clea was in there.…

A uniformed guard, almost as wide as he was tall, blocked the entrance, and his scrutiny reminded Brand that in his haste to see Clea he had yet to don the rented tuxedo jacket still slung across his left arm.

Brand's mouth slanted in a wry grimace. What would the man have thought of the battered fatigues he'd worn for the better part of four years?

Impatience and anticipation ratcheted up another notch, and the ache to see Clea—hold her, kiss her—consumed him.

Breaking into a lope, Brand headed for the glass doors, shrugging on the dinner jacket as he went. He pulled the collar straight and smoothed down the satin lapels with scarred and callused fingertips. As the security guard examined the invitations of the group in front, Brand tagged on behind the tail-enders. To his relief, the guard waved him through with the rest of the party.

He'd negotiated the first barrier.

Now to find Clea…

Brand would've loved the tiger.

As always, the sight of the stone figure transfixed Clea. The chatter and clinking of champagne glasses faded away as she studied the powerful feline. Crafted by a Sumerian stone carver eons ago, the leashed power of the piece was compelling, calling to her on a primal level that she could not explain.

Without question Brand would have loved it. That had been her very first thought when she'd spotted the half life-size cat eighteen months earlier—she'd had to have it. Convincing Alan Daley, the museum's head curator, and the acquisition board to acquire it had taken some doing;

the financial outlay had been considerable. But the statue had proved to be a crowd pleaser.

And it was inexorably linked in her mind to Brand, serving as a daily memorial to her husband.

Her late husband.

"Clea?"

The voice that broke into her thoughts was softer than Brand's rough velvet tones. Not Brand, but Harry…

Brand was dead. Tossed without honor into some mass grave in the hot, dry desert of Iraq. Years of unending questions, desperate prayers and daily flashes of hope were finally over. Ended, irrevocably, in the most unwelcome manner nine months ago.

But he would never be forgotten. Clea had vowed to make certain of that.

Determinedly shrugging off the shroud of melancholy, she brushed a curl off her face and turned away from the statue to her father's business associate and her oldest friend. "Yes, Harry?"

Harry Hall-Lewis set his hands on her shoulders and gazed down at her. "Yes? Now that's the word I've been waiting a long time to hear you say."

The playful note in his tone caused Clea to roll her eyes. How she wished he'd tire of the game he'd made of the arranged-marriage plan their fathers had hatched for them two decades ago. "Not now, Harry." On cue her phone beeped.

Relieved, she extracted her cell phone from her clutch and glanced at it. "It's Dad." As chairman of the museum's board of trustees, Donald Tomlinson had been giving prospective patrons a private tour of the exhibit.

After listening to her father for a few moments, Clea hung up and said to Harry, "He's finished the tour, and yes, he has secured more funding. He wants us to come join him."

"You're changing the subject." Harry's hands tightened momentarily on her bare shoulders, making Clea aware of the brevity of the bodice of her floor-length gown. Then the moment of self-consciousness was gone as Harry released her from the friendly hold with a chuckle. "One day I'll convince you to marry me. And that will be the day you realize what you've been missing all these years."

Clea stepped back, unaccountably needing a little distance from him. "Oh, Harry, that joke wore thin a long time ago."

The humor evaporated from his face.

"Is the thought of marrying me so repulsive?"

His hangdog expression added to her guilt. They'd grown up together. Their fathers had been best friends; in all ways that mattered Harry was the brother she'd never had. Why couldn't he understand that she needed him in that role, not as the husband their fathers had cast him as decades ago?

Gently touching the sleeve of his tailored jacket, she said, "Oh, Harry, you're my best friend, I love you dearly—"

"I sense a *but* coming."

The winking glitter from the chandeliers overhead gave his eyes an unnatural sparkle. Despite his carefree persona, Harry had always been perceptive. And he was right, there was a *but*. A great big, tall, dark and heartbreakingly absent *but*.

Brand…

The love of her life…and utterly irreplaceable. Grief had created a black void in her life that drained her of joy. How she missed him!

Clea shut off the line of thought that always led to

unstanched pain and wild regret, and focused instead on Harry. "I'm just not ready to think of marriage again."

She doubted she'd ever be ready.

"Surely you don't still harbor hope that Brand is alive?"

Harry's words caused the frenetic buzz that had been driving her for months to subside, forcing her to confront the pain she'd so carefully kept from facing. Weariness—and a lonely longing—overtook her. All at once Clea wished she was home, alone in the bedroom she'd once shared with Brand, cocooned in the comfort of their bed. The familiar ache of loss swamped her.

Dropping her hand from Harry's sleeve, she wrapped her arms around her tummy and said in a high, thin voice, "This is the wrong time for this discussion."

Harry caught her arm and said quietly, "Clea, for the past nine months, since you received confirmation that Brand is dead, you *never* want to talk about him."

Clea flinched at the reminder of that awful day.

"I know you did everything in your power to find him, Clea, that you never gave up hoping that he was alive. But he's not. He's dead, and probably has been for over four years—however much you tried to deny it. You have to accept it."

"I know he's—" her voice broke "—dead."

Harry looked as shocked by her disjointed statement as she felt.

Coldness crept through her.

Defeated, Clea's shoulders drooped and the soft satin of the sea-green dress—the color of Brand's eyes—sagged around her body. She shivered, suddenly chilled despite the warm summer evening.

It was the first time she'd admitted Brand's death out loud.

For so long she'd refused to stop hoping. She'd prayed.

She'd kept the flame of faith alive deep in her heart, in that sacred place only Brand had ever touched. Clea had even convinced herself that if Brand had been dead a piece of her soul would have withered. So all through the months—the years—of waiting she'd stubbornly refused to extinguish the last flicker of hope. Not even when her father and friends were telling her to face reality: Brand wasn't coming back.

Harry spoke, breaking into her thoughts. "Well, accepting he's dead is a major step forward."

"Harry—"

"Look, I know it's been a tough time for you. Those first days of silence." Harry shook his head. "And then discovering he'd gone to Baghdad with another woman—"

"I might've been wrong about Brand still being alive," Clea interrupted heatedly, "but Brand was *not* having an affair with Anita Freeman—I don't care what the investigators say." Clea wouldn't tolerate having her memory of Brand defiled. "It's not true. Their minds belong in some Baghdad sewer."

"But your father—"

"I don't care what Dad thinks, I absolutely refuse to believe it. Besides we both know Dad never cared much for Brand. Let it rest." She hesitated. "Brand and Anita were colleagues."

"Colleagues?" Harry's voice was loaded with innuendo.

"Okay, they dated a few times. But it was over before Brand met me." How Clea hated this. The way the gossip tarnished the love she and Brand had shared.

"That might have been what Brand wanted you to believe. But the investigators found proof that they'd lived together for over a year in London before he met you— hell, that's longer than he was married to you, Clea. Why did he never mention that? Your husband died in a car crash with the woman in the Iraq desert. Stop deceiving yourself!"

A quick scan around revealed no one close enough to overhear their conversation. Thank God. Clea stepped closer and spoke in a low tone: "They did not live together—Brand would've told me that. The relationship was brief. They only kept contact because of work. Brand was an antiquities expert, Anita was an archaeologist. Of course they ran across each other."

"But you'll never know for sure. Because Brand never even told you he was going to Iraq."

Unable to argue with Harry's logic, Clea straightened and said, "I have no intention of conducting a postmortem on this."

Her husband was dead. It was tragic enough that her bone-deep conviction that he'd been out there some-where—hurting...maybe suffering memory loss...waiting to be found—had been misguided.

But then, everyone had always thought she was mad to hope he might still be alive in the face of the mounting evidence that he must be dead. The burned-out wreck of Brand's rented vehicle had been found in the desert, and nearby villagers had confirmed burying the charred remains of a man and a woman in a local mass grave.

Despite the investigators' certainty that Brand had perished in the desert, Clea had wanted proof. That it had indeed been Brand who had died, not someone else. Not even the fact that no one had seen or heard from Brand since his disappearance or the fact that his bank accounts had remained untouched could quell her hopes.

But nine months ago, after years of lingering hope, Clea had received the proof she'd dreaded.

Brand's wedding ring. Stolen off one of the corpses

by a member of the burial team and later turning up in a pawnbroker's stall at the local village market.

Brand would never have taken his ring off. *Never.* Finally, no choice remained but to face the truth: Brand had died in that wreck in the desert. He was not coming back.

Her beloved husband was dead.

There'd been nothing left for her to do but complete the formalities.

The court accepted what her father, the investigating team and the lawyers dispassionately called "the facts" and made an order confirming that Brand was dead, authorizing a death certificate to be issued.

The day she'd received the death certificate, the final document charting Brand's life, Clea's heart had shattered into glass-sharp fragments. She'd believed she would never come to terms with the harsh finality of it.

Harry's familiar features became a blur as her vision teared up. Yet amid the ashes of despair she'd found a way to combat her loneliness...

"Now I've upset you." Harry looked more wretched than ever. "I never meant to do that."

"It's not you."

Clea blinked furiously. How could she explain that everything made her feel tearful? The doctor said that was normal—it would pass.

"It's me. I'm just all over the place right now."

That caused Harry to take a hurried step back.

Patting the front of his dinner jacket, Clea gave a wan smile. "It's okay, I promise I won't bawl my eyes out."

Harry gave a hasty glance around, then said gamely, "You can cry on my shoulder anytime you want."

Her throat ached. "I'm done crying. I know—and accept—that Brand is dead. I know that I have to move on. Everything is going to be all right." If she told herself that often enough she might one day start believing it. For good measure she added, "And I've got something to live for."

"Clea, if you need me—I'll be there for you. You know that."

Yet despite his brave words Harry looked so alarmed by the prospect of her falling apart here, in front of New York's high society, that Clea couldn't help smiling. "Harry, thank you. You're the best."

Relief lit Harry's expression. "Isn't that what friends are for?"

In the foyer of the Museum of Ancient Antiquities, Brand paused midstep and looked around. It was different from the last time he'd been here...yet still very familiar.

Dated black-and-white tiles had given way to glossy white marble. And the flooring wasn't the only change. An imposing, curved marble staircase with an ornate bronze balustrade wound upward in the space once occupied by creaky wooden stairs covered in threadbare, mustard-colored carpeting from the 1950s. To the right of the stairs, a magnificent bronze immortalized a pre-Christian goddess. The wreath of corn she wore allowed Brand to identify her as Inanna, the ancient Mesopotamian goddess of love, fertility and war.

The dark, old-fashioned entrance hall had been transformed into a sophisticated, inviting space just as Clea had sketched one snowy winter's evening while they'd reclined beside the glowing fire at home. Brand had listened as she'd shared a vision of how the museum could become New York's most exciting collection of ancient treasures.

Brand moved forward slowly.

A rush of pride filled him. His wife had clearly accomplished what she'd once only dreamed of. The museum was no longer a somewhat dowdy haunt of scholars and art aficionados. It was thriving…alive… exactly as she'd envisaged.

At the foot of the stairs a flock of women in high heels and designer frocks were being served oversize cosmopolitans by a white-jacketed waiter.

There was a buzz of excitement in the air.

Brand's gaze searched the group.

No Clea. Beyond the fashionistas lurked more clusters of people. His gaze sharpened. Men. All of them. Formally clad in black-and-white and scattered beneath the bronze of Inanna.

Where was his wife?

His heart hammering, Brand advanced, passing under a gilded chandelier, its iridescent crystals dispersing flecks of light across the domed arch of the ceiling far above. He made for the spectacular staircase he knew must lead to the second floor and the upper galleries. He couldn't wait to watch Clea's incredible green eyes light up with unrestrained joy when she saw him, couldn't wait to touch her, feel her soft warmth, her femininity within his arms. How he'd dreamed of that.

His wife. His lover. His lodestar. Every minute away from her had almost killed him.

Reaching the top of the stairs, Brand paused. The long gallery was crowded. The sparkle of jewels and riot of color was blinding. He fought an unexpected wave of claustrophobia as the crowd enveloped him.

Perhaps he should've called ahead, let her know he was coming home….

But with the worst of the long and dangerous trek through the mountains bordering northern Iraq behind him, he'd wanted to get the less risky journey back to the United States done. Sure, there'd still been the chance that he could be arrested for carrying a fake passport. And, beneath reason, there'd lurked the blind terror that calling Clea might jinx everything.

Too late for second thoughts now.

Brand scanned the throng crammed between glass display cases holding priceless ancient treasures and tables loaded with canapés. Still no sight of the woman he sought. He edged past a trio of gossiping older women, their hungry eyes incessantly sweeping the packed room for fresh fodder before they turned to each other and cackled. His lips started to curl…then relaxed into a rusty smile. In the past he would've dismissed them as social hyenas; but now, after his months of deprivation, any laughter was a welcome sound.

He met the heavily mascaraed eyes of one of the group. Saw the disbelief as recognition dawned. Marcia Mercer. Brand remembered that she used to pen an influential society column. Perhaps she still did.

"Brand…Brand Noble?"

He gave her a nod in brief acknowledgment before advancing with ruthless determination, ignoring the turning heads, the growing babble that followed in his wake.

And then he saw her.

Brand's mouth went dry. The cacophony of rising voices faded. There was only Clea…

She was smiling.

Her mouth curved up, and her eyes sparkled. A shimmering ball gown clung to her curves, her arms bare except for a gold cuff that glowed in the light from the opulent chandeliers…and on her left hand the wedding band he'd chosen for her glinted.

Brand sucked in his breath.

For an instant he thought she'd cut off the riot of curls he loved. But as she turned her head he caught a glimpse of curls escaping down behind her back from where the dark tresses had been pulled away from her face. He let out the breath he hadn't been aware of holding in a jagged groan. She looked so vital, so alive and so stunningly beautiful.

Longing surged through him and his chest expanded into an ache too complex to identify.

Clea's hand reached out and touched a jacketed arm. Brand's gaze followed. The sight of the bronze-haired man she was touching caused Brand's eyes to narrow dangerously. So Harry Hall-Lewis was still around. When she tipped her face up and directed the full blast of her smile at the man, Brand wanted to yank Clea away. To pull her to him, hold her, never let her go.

Mine.

The response roared through him. Basic, primal…and very, very male.

"Champagne, sir?"

The waiter's interruption broke his concentration on Clea. Brand helped himself to a glass from the tray with hands that shook, and he gulped the golden liquid down to moisten his tight, parched throat.

Then he set the empty glass down and drew a steadying breath.

He had his life back…and he had no intention of spending another moment away from the woman who had lured him back from beyond the darkness with the memory of her smile.

There was no time to waste.

Yet, when he looked across the room again, Clea and her companion had vanished.

* * *

After a terse exchange with her father near the Egyptian room, Clea then sneaked behind a tall pillar while Harry ventured into the crowd to fetch her a drink. Leaning against the cool column, she shut her eyes. If her father saw her he'd lecture her about duty, about the importance of networking and getting out in front of all the television cameras in attendance. Clea pursed her mouth in a moue of resignation. Of course he was right. But she needed a little time alone. She wasn't in the mood for small talk, and the growing whispers were causing the latent tension within her to spiral out of control.

"Clea."

That voice. She jerked around like a puppet on a string, eyes stretched wide, shock punching the air out of her lungs.

Breathless, she whispered, "Brand...?"

It couldn't be. Disbelief made her blink. *Brand was dead.*

The man coming toward her was tall, dark and very much alive.

A ghost from the past.

Heat seared her, instantly followed by an icy chill. He was a dead ringer for her very dead husband—the man she'd officially had declared dead eight months ago, a month after being given his ring back.

This was cruel. Brand was gone. Forever. Hadn't she spent the past nine months trying to come to terms with the final proof of his death after nearly four years of terrible, traumatic uncertainty?

Blood rushed to her head. The sudden airlessness of the room pressed in on her.

Clea couldn't breathe, and she felt horribly ill. Her father would never forgive her if she was sick all over the marble floor…with press cameras everywhere to immortalize the moment.

"Clea!"

The hands that came down on her shoulders were so intimately familiar…yet so painfully strange. She shook her head, resisting the cold mist closing in on her. *He was dead.* Yet the fingers cupping her shoulders were warm, strong and very much alive.

This was no ghost.

This was a human being. A man she knew too well.

"Don't faint on me," he warned in that deep, slightly hoarse voice.

"I won't." She'd never fainted in her life. Yet she had to admit that she felt weak, dizzy…dazed. "You're supposed to be dead!" She sucked in a ragged breath, and then added inanely, "But you're back."

Clea!

A raw, burning hunger he hadn't experienced for more than a thousand nights overpowered Brand. He pulled the woman he'd dreamed of every day—every night—toward him, drinking in the scent of her, a heady mix of honey and jasmine. He closed his eyes and inhaled deeply. Her warmth and fragrance flooded him.

Beneath the exploring pads of his fingers her shoulders were more slender than he remembered, the bones fragile, but her skin was as soft as ever. "You've lost weight."

She stiffened under his touch. "Maybe."

Brand buried his face in the side of her neck, iron bands of emotion constricting his chest.

"I've missed you," he breathed, "so much." Without her, a void had replaced the man he'd been. His arms tightened around her slender frame, words pouring from him, rough guttural sounds against her smooth skin.

"Brand, I can't hear you." Clea drew away a little. "It's too loud in here—let's find somewhere quieter."

She slipped out of his hold and a sense of loss swamped Brand.

Clea held out a hand. "Come."

He took the fingers she offered, the delicate link frighteningly fragile.

She pulled him along with her, threading between the press of staring people until they broke clear, escaping through open double doors into a carpeted corridor beyond. Clea halted outside a set of glass doors in the clear floor-to-ceiling glass wall. Letting go of his hand, she fished in her evening purse looped over her shoulder by a delicate chain and extracted a keycard, which she swiped in the security slot. The doors sprang open and Brand followed her into a reception area and the corridor beyond. "My office is through here."

Brand paused. "You used to be down in the basement."

Her chin tilted up in a gesture that was pure Clea, and his heart clenched.

"I've moved up in the world," she told him, her eyes hungrily searching his face. "I'm more important now."

Clea pressed a wall switch and light flooded the room, catching forgotten glints of precious copper in her long, dark curls, hinting at the fire that lay beneath.

Lust caught him by the throat.

He'd missed her so damn much. Missed talking to her. Missed touching her.

Most of all he'd missed loving her.

Clea.

In a flash, Brand closed the space between them and took her in his arms again. He couldn't get enough of touching her, reassuring himself that she was here, in his hold. Not a wraith that would vanish with his dreams as dawn cracked over the endless, empty horizon. Bending his head, he slanted his lips across hers. She gave a surprised gasp, and a beat later melted into his embrace.

She tasted so sweet, and his hunger soared.

Tracing the indent of her spine with shaking fingers, Brand's hands moved up...up...until his fingers speared into the soft, glossy mass of constrained curls. Her head fell back and he deepened the kiss.

Her breasts pressed against his chest, and despite her weight loss they seemed fuller than he remembered. Clea had always bemoaned her lack of curves, but now she was positively lush.

Another change.

But this one he would savor...

He brought his hands forward to shape her ripe flesh and his fingers skimmed her belly. Fuller there, too. A curious anomaly given the slenderness of her shoulders, the sharp definition of her high cheekbones. His hands rested on the rise, his fingers exploring...and he felt her still.

Blood roared in Brand's ears. He couldn't absorb what his fingertips were telling him.

No!

His first reaction was denial. But his hands had developed a life—a reasoning power—all their own, even as his mind sputtered then stalled. His palms stroked over Clea's curves, sending bursts of unwelcome information back to his struggling brain until he could no longer deny the truth of what lay beneath his hands.

Raising his head, he glared accusingly down into her startled green eyes. "You're pregnant!"

Two

Clea knew at once how it must appear.

"It's not what you think," she said quickly, reaching up to cradle Brand's beloved face between her cupped hands. "Remember how we—"

"It certainly didn't take you long to find someone else."

The blaze of accusation rocked her. Brand had gone all tense, his jaw clenching and unclenching against her hollowed palms as he glowered at her from between slitted lids.

In the stillness of her office, Clea stared up at him in absolute shock, the awfulness of what he was saying— what he believed—finally sinking in.

There was no one else.

"I didn't—"

"Shut up," he snarled.

"Wait a minute…"

Clea's voiced trailed away as his hands manacled her

wrists. He forced her fingers away from his skin and
dropped them with palpable distaste, and all the while
the beautiful ocean-hued eyes bored unblinkingly into
hers. "It didn't take you long to accept that I was dead—
or was it a case of out of sight, out of mind?"

The injustice of that caused her to reel away, almost
tripping over the visitor's chair in front of her desk. Clea
sank onto the padded black leather, her legs weak.

How *could* Brand believe that?

Especially when she'd never stopped believing in him!

Five days after her last telephone conversation with
Brand, unable to contact him, Clea had sounded the alarm.
It had taken another thirteen days—the longest stretch of
Clea's life—for the official channels to relay back to her
that Brand was no longer in Greece. He'd entered Iraq
over two weeks earlier through the Kuwait border and had
checked into a battle-scarred hotel once favored by foreign
businessmen in Baghdad. No one knew where he'd gone
after checking out a few days later.

There had been nothing left to do but wait. She'd made
every excuse in the book for him. But time passed and still
he hadn't gotten in touch.

To the men in black suits who materialized like spooks
at her workplace Clea had insisted there had been nothing
suspicious about her husband's visit to Iraq; after all, Brand
made his living from dealing in antiquities, a love he'd
developed while stationed with the Australian Special Air
Services elite forces in Iraq. But it had been galling to
admit that he hadn't told her about his intention to enter
Iraq, and she decided not to tell her visitors about the
argument she'd had with Brand the second to last time
she'd spoken to him.

Once the shadowy men in black suits departed, on her

father's advice and using his extensive contacts, Clea had hired a firm of investigators to locate her missing husband.

It had *never* been a case of out of sight, out of mind.

She hadn't stopped thinking about him, not for one minute. Even the two identical clocks on her office wall bore testimony to that—one set to Eastern Time, the other to Baghdad time. She'd never stopped thinking what he might be doing at any moment of her day. She'd wanted her husband back. She'd wanted answers about his disappearance. Real answers. Not speculation that he'd deserted her for another woman, which had been the first theory the investigators had come up with. The news of the grisly discovery of the burned-out SUV in the desert had terrified her. But she'd stubbornly clung to her belief that she would've known in her heart if Brand was dead. She'd demanded incontrovertible proof.

When they'd brought her his wedding ring nine months ago, Clea had been shattered, her dreams pulverized to dust, her hopes charred to ashes.

The idea of a baby had become a lifeline to sanity.

Getting pregnant had given her back her life. Not the life she'd hoped to share with Brand, but something better than the hopelessness that had overtaken her.

Yet now Brand stood over her accusing *her* of forgetting *him*. Instead of taking her in his arms, he was behaving like the world's biggest bastard. And he showed no signs of listening anytime soon. Clea shook her head to clear it and pressed her hands protectively over her stomach.

Brand laughed—a harsh, grating sound she'd never heard before. "Nothing further to say? How unfortunate for you I didn't remain dead." The sea-green gaze had turned arctic.

Slumped in the chair, Clea's whole body ached. Her feet.

Her head. Her heart. Was it possible Brand was hurting every bit as much as she was? "I can explain…"

Brand recoiled.

"I don't need your explanations!" He looked down on her from the full height of his six-foot-two-inch frame. His eyes froze her out. "It's easy enough to see what happened." One side of his mouth kicked up. "So who's the lucky man?"

"Will you stop interrupting me?" Her voice rose. Hauling in a shaky breath, she tempered her tone. "We always talked about having a family—"

"*Our* family," he said, pointedly inspecting her belly, covered by the silk of her designer dress and sheltered by her clasped hands. "Not some other man's bastard."

"Brand, wait!"

Clea rose to her feet and reached for him, then dropped her hands to her sides at the icy look he bestowed on her.

"Please listen—"

"What's the point of listening?" There was contempt in the frigid gaze that met hers, and something else…

Disappointment?

His lack of faith stung. She deserved a chance to explain, and she didn't doubt that he'd listen once he'd calmed down. Brand might have a dangerous reputation, but he loved her.

Or did he?

The first shadow of doubt stole over her. Clea stilled. She'd always imagined that something terrible must've happened to keep him away for so long. A horrific accident. Memory loss. Trauma so terrible he hadn't wanted her to see him in such a state.

Instead he stood before her looking breathtakingly hunky in the tuxedo and black shirt, his body even better conditioned than four years earlier—some feat because

Brand had always honed his body to perfection. His face was burnished bronze by the sun, contrasting with the color of his sea-green eyes to devastating effect. An aura of reckless danger now clung to him, causing her heart to beat faster.

He might not be the Brand she'd kissed goodbye at the airport—but he wasn't damaged or scarred.

Yet she had to admit, dressed all in black, he looked like the devil incarnate.

Without taking her eyes from him, she toed off her shoes, adding another two inches to the height advantage he already possessed. "So why didn't you tell me you were going to Baghdad?" she challenged.

Brand stared back at her.

Did he cause Anita Freeman's heart to beat faster, too? "Answer me!"

Nothing. Not even a blink. He simply kept watching her with that basilisk stare she was starting to loathe.

"I've waited—"

A brow lifted ironically at that. "Waited?"

"Yes! *Waited.*" Clea pushed a tendril back off her face. "The last decent conversation we shared, you were in London—about to go to Greece. We argued about that. Remember?" She'd wanted to rearrange her schedule and had asked Brand to wait until she could join him. He'd refused—and ordered her to stay home. Clea hadn't taken kindly to being so summarily dismissed. It wasn't the first time that Brand had made decisions for her. She'd sulked. He'd called her once more from Athens—and their conversation had been stilted and brief. Just before he'd cut the connection, he'd told her he loved her.

Then there'd been no more contact.

When he didn't respond, she said, "You never told me you planned to go to Iraq."

His gaze didn't waver. "I didn't want to worry you."

Could the explanation really be that simple? Or had the business trip to Greece been a cover for an affair with another woman? Had the investigators' first theory—supported by her father and Harry—been correct after all?

The ticking of the two wall clocks was the only sound in the room.

Clea broke the silence. "That's all? That's the reason you never mentioned it?" If she hadn't been watching him so closely, Clea might have missed the sideways flicker of his eyes.

Brand wasn't telling her the truth.

Or at least not the whole truth.

The silence stretched until Clea broke it. "Don't you think concern that you might be maimed or kidnapped or even killed would be a reasonable reaction to being told that you were going to Baghdad?"

He shrugged, his broad shoulders flexing under the tuxedo, causing her gaze to stray for a brief moment before returning to his face. "I served there with the SAS," he said. "I know the territory—and the risks."

Frustration and a feeling of letdown drove her to sarcasm. "Okay, so those risks might not worry super-humans like you…but they sure do worry me."

"Which is exactly why I didn't tell you—I didn't have time to soothe you."

Like some clingy child. But this was getting interesting. Brand was lying to her. Clea was certain of it. His face wore a set expression, and his eyes had flicked away again. "So what was so important that you simply went without consulting me? And why no contact since? Surely you can't have been in Baghdad all this time?"

He resumed staring at her, tight-lipped.

Clea tried again. "Were you on some covert mission?"

He laughed at that, making her feel ridiculously melo-dramatic. Yet she couldn't help thinking of the dark-suited men who had surfaced after his disappearance and asked her why he'd gone to Baghdad—and seemed to know all about his special forces background.

"At least tell me it's classified, if that's the reason."

"I wasn't part of a military operation."

She deserved more than being stonewalled. Drawing a deep breath, Clea eased back against her glass-topped desk and said, "Tell me where you've been, and I'll consider explaining about the baby…on condition that you don't interrupt me until I've told you everything."

"I don't need your conditions—or your explanations," he said. A look followed that slashed her from head to toe—with significant focus on her almost-flat stomach. "I can see exactly what you've been up to."

Brand might not need explanations, but she sure as hell did.

Yet Clea wasn't about to let him see how much she cared. Not while he treated her like a leper. Instead she gave him a reciprocal once-over, taking in every inch of tanned skin and the trim body beneath the tuxedo, and then she pursed her lips. "Let me guess where you've been. Sunning yourself on the Mediterranean? Socializing with the Aga Khan?"

Sleeping with another woman? Clea was too terrified of his response to voice the last suspicion. But was it possible that her father and the investigators had been correct? That Brand had been having an affair? Was it possible that Brand had been living with his lover for the four years he'd gone missing without a trace? He certainly possessed the skills to remain undetected for as long as he wanted—if he wanted.

Brand's face had tightened. "You've developed a sharp tongue."

"Now it's my fault?"

What was she doing?

Clea shut her eyes. Why was she fighting with Brand? This wasn't what she wanted. Remorse washed over her and she shook her head to clear it of the turmoil and confusion, searching for calm. How had it all gone so wrong so quickly? This was Brand. She *loved* him. She'd always believed in him. She'd waited for him to return every day. Every night. Yet now that he was here she was hurting so much she could spit...and doubts were setting in.

They had to stop this.

She fisted her hands at her sides and drew in a ragged breath. When she was certain she had herself under control—that she wouldn't yell, or blubber like an idiot— she opened her eyes and said evenly, "Sorry, I didn't mean to sound like a shrew."

His closed expression didn't thaw. Her body strung tight, Clea wished desperately he would confess he'd been injured, hospitalized, that he'd temporarily lost his memory. Anything.

The silence wore thin.

Still she waited, her hands balled tight and her pulse pounding loudly in her ears. Waiting for an explanation of where he'd been, why he'd stayed away so long. Clea even convinced herself that she'd accept it without question, without revealing a hint of resentment for what he'd *dared* to put her through. Brand was back, and that would be enough. Wouldn't it? She *loved* him. She'd only been half-alive without him. She couldn't allow his return to break her, when she'd already survived his disappearance...and his death.

But as the minute hands on the wall clocks pressed forward in tandem, Clea gave up.

Brand wasn't going to explain.

Why not?

Because he no longer cared?

Only one way to find out.

"Brand…" Clea unfurled her fists and stepped away from the safety of her desk. Standing on tiptoes, she reached up and placed her hands on his shoulders, searching for a connection. Under the black silk of his dress shirt she could feel the warmth of his skin. She flexed her fingertips. His muscles bunched in reaction.

Need—hot and unexpected—hollowed out the bottom of her stomach. *God, she'd missed him.* His remembered scent—a mix of musk and something sharp and tangy— filled her senses.

Shutting her eyes, she leaned into him, her body quivering as it came into contact with the taut length of his. The warmth of his big body seeped gradually into hers, reviving her after the heart-numbing chill. For a long moment she half dared to hope that their bodies might communicate even while their brains seemed estranged.

The baby moved.

And even as her lips brushed his chin, Brand tore out of her embrace.

Putting two yards between them, he came to a stop near the doorway, breathing heavily, his eyes glittering, the golden skin stretched taut across his cheekbones.

"What the hell is the matter with you?" Clea tried never to swear, but the force with which he wrenched away offended her. This time *she* wasn't going to close the distance between them.

"You need to ask?"

Clea resented being treated as if she were contaminated.

Her thoughts flew to the baby. She was pregnant, not contagious. Her condition was her salvation.

"Yes!" She *did* need to ask. And she was prepared to listen to—and accept—any explanation he cared to make for his absence. But he wasn't prepared to extend her the same courtesy. It looked as if they'd finally reached a deadlock. Because as her ire grew, Clea was finding herself less willing to offer him any explanation until he showed her the respect and trust she deserved.

"What the hell does it matter what's with me?" His voice was flat and cold. "Whatever we once had is gone."

"Gone?" At that her heart bumped to a stop. Forgetting her resolve to keep away, Clea took a step closer and stared at him in horror. "Brand! You don't—*can't*—mean that."

"Yes, gone." He raked her with his ocean-blue gaze. But for once, rather than setting her alight with sensual, arousing heat, it froze her to the core. "It's been a long time. Too long, I suspect, for us to have kept what we once had."

Pain ripped through her. Clea's world came crashing down around her as she struggled to sort the thoughts crowding her brain into some kind of order. *Had* Brand been unfaithful? Had he come back only to claim a divorce?

Cold emptiness settled in her stomach. Clea was starting to realize that her steadfast belief in Brand had been awfully naive.

"Did you ever live with Anita Freeman?" She blurted it out with no premeditation.

"What does that have to do with anything?"

"You dated her."

He stood, unmoving. "For a time."

"A short time?"

"Why these questions about something that was over before we met?"

Clea's brain was working overtime. Brand was prevaricating. He hadn't wanted her with him in Greece; without consulting her, he'd gone to a country he knew she would deem too dangerous. According to the investigators, both times Anita had been with him. In Athens they'd been photographed together and witnesses that the investigators had spoken with had seen them together in Baghdad. They'd appeared inseparable.

At the time Clea had refused to believe him capable of that kind of treachery. Brand loved *her*.

The last words he'd spoken to her had been that he loved her—but she hadn't reciprocated. She'd been annoyed with him for turning down the opportunity for a romantic idyll in Greece. Okay, so perhaps it was her own guilt that had prevented her from facing the truth earlier, Clea decided wearily.

Had his avowal of love been motivated by guilt? Had she blamed herself on some unconscious level for his disappearance because she'd been sulking the last time they'd talked?

Finally, she said, "I want to know if you ever lived with her." She already suspected what his answer would be: Brand had lied in the past.

His mouth slashed down in displeasure.

He wasn't even bothering to deny it. The last bit of hope she hadn't even realized she was clinging to deserted Clea.

"Who told you I once lived with Anita?" Brand broke into her despair.

"Does it matter? By your reaction I take it that it must be true. Why lead me to believe it was nothing more than a couple of casual dates? You lied to me by omission."

"So in retaliation you went and cheated on me and got yourself pregnant?"

Clea's mouth fell open. "You have the gall to walk in here after an absence of four years and accuse *me* of cheating on *you*."

"You're pregnant," Brand snarled. "And I sure as hell haven't been around to give you a good time."

The force of his harsh words caused tears to prick. Clea bit her cheeks until it hurt and the tears dried up. She half wished she'd never started down this track. But, after years of stubborn denial, admitting her stupidity and acknowledging that Brand had been with someone else was hard.

Whatever we once had is gone.

For now that was all she needed to know. Brand had made his choice.

Choking back tears, Clea slipped her feet back into her shoes then headed blindly for the door. As she drew level with Brand, she braced herself and said with the last shred of dignity she could muster, "Maybe you'll be prepared to tell me more once you've had a chance to think. Close my office door when you leave…it will latch behind you. This is an important night for me, and I'm going to celebrate my success."

Clea edged past him, taking care not to brush against him.

And Brand didn't try to stop her.

Three

"Bourbon, double on ice. Your order?"

Brand gave a curt nod in acknowledgment of the barman's question and reached for the heavy-bottomed glass, while keeping a wary eye on the gaggle of journalists who'd shown a great deal of interest since he'd reentered the gallery.

The first slug hit the back of his throat. Brand grimaced. In four years he'd forgotten the punch that whiskey packed. Picking up the pitcher on the bar counter, Brand added two fingers of water to the bourbon.

Glass in hand, he retreated to a deserted spot behind a column topped with a woman's head carved from marble to sip his drink. Out of sight of the media contingent, Brand searched for his errant wife. He located her in a group that included a senator, the senator's wife and a well-known art auctioneer. As he studied Clea, he tried to fathom why he hadn't already departed.

With the media about to erupt into full bay at his mysterious reappearance any moment, it made no sense to still be hanging around. Not unless he wished to make front-page news…and that had never been Brand's style.

Clea's laugh rang out and Brand stilled, his eyebrows jerking together. She looked vivacious and happy— not as if she'd just had a rip-roaring argument with the husband she hadn't seen for four years. Clearly at ease in the company of power, she'd developed a poise and sophistication she hadn't possessed four years ago.

His wife had grown up. He'd left a young bride and come back to find a woman. Brand's gaze dropped to her stomach.

Make that a *pregnant* woman.

Her father joined the group. Brand's frown deepened as the senator welcomed Donald Tomlinson with a wide smile. When they'd first met, Clea had told him her father would love him—after all, they had much in common. Donald Tomlinson imported rugs, ceramics, wooden furniture and selected antiquities from Afghanistan, Iraq and Turkey for a string of up-market stores he owned. Clea considered it a miracle they hadn't already encountered each other.

Brand had known from their first handshake that Donald Tomlinson didn't care for him. Meeting Clea's childhood friend had explained why—Harry Hall-Lewis was the man Donald had singled out for his daughter to marry. Ivy League-educated, a successful import-exporter with whom her father had a close business relationship, Harry was affable and easygoing. That Harry's family could trace their genealogy back to the *Mayflower* also helped.

An ex-special forces soldier from a rural New Zealand family of no repute could hardly compete, regardless of the reputation for integrity he'd built—or his rapidly growing fortune based on the ever-escalating value of the ancient artifacts he dealt in. Millions meant little to Donald—he had enough of his own. When Clea had chosen a hasty marriage in Las Vegas's Chapel of Love to her soldier-turned-antiquities-dealer, Donald's displeasure had become outright enmity.

"Brand...it *is* you. How wonderful. Where have you been?"

Brand turned his head. Clea's mother stood beside him, her dark hair swept into a chignon, her black dress timelessly elegant. Diamonds glittered at her throat. He'd only encountered Caroline a handful of times during his marriage to Clea. The only child of a wealthy industrialist, Caroline had walked out on her marriage to Donald when Clea had been ten years old and remarried soon after her divorce had come through. A successful businessman, her new husband was a widower with a daughter—the same age as Clea—and a younger son.

"It's been a while." Brand gave her a careful hug. After so long without close human contact it felt strange. "You look beautiful."

"Flatterer." Caroline Fraser Tomlinson Gordon hugged him back, before stepping away with a small smile. "You look surprised to see me here. Of course, you should be—I wasn't invited. I had the sense not to bring my husband, but I wanted to see Cleopatra's exhibition so I slipped in— the doorman told me I had the same eyes as Cleopatra and never considered refusing me entrance. I've been admiring the exhibits. She's done a magnificent job. I'm so proud of her." Caroline's emerald eyes shimmered with emotion.

Omitting to mention that he was also a gate-crasher, Brand said gently, "You ought to have been invited."

Brand suspected that the estrangement between Clea

and her mother hurt Clea more than she'd ever admit. She had always craved family and she needed her mother—even though she was too stubborn to admit it.

"My daughter will never forgive me for leaving them."

Brand shifted uncomfortably. There was no tactful response to that. Finally, he settled for saying, "She needs you, she just doesn't know it yet. Give her time."

At a scuffling sound behind him, he turned his head a fraction. His peripheral vision caught sight of a newsman changing the lens of his camera.

He turned away. Afghanistan, Iraq and other hot spots during his days of active duty had taught him the game. There was no glory in a back-of-the-head view: Cameramen wanted to see the torment in the eyes of their prey.

Caroline said quietly, "Cleopatra must know you're back?"

"Yes." Brand's answer was clipped as he focused on what the cameraman's next move might be.

His mother-in-law tapped his jacket sleeve. "Brand, you know I've never been in her confidence, but I do know she missed you terribly after you…disappeared. The weight that fell off her was evidence enough."

Her eyes were full of questions. Questions that he couldn't—wouldn't—answer. Not yet.

He gestured to where Clea was talking and smiling. "So much that she's pregnant?"

"Pregnant?" Caroline examined her daughter's figure. "Cleopatra?"

Brand scanned the crowd. The cameraman had disappeared, but two others were hunched together talking furtively. "Uh-huh."

"She can't be!"

He turned his attention back to Clea's mother and bent forward. "Trust me, she is."

Caroline had paled. "I didn't even know she was seeing anyone. But why would Cleopatra tell me? We don't talk."

Brand heard the movement beside him, and then a light flashed. He ducked his head and retreated farther behind the pillar. Someone swore softly.

Another movement. Brand tensed. He had no compunction about breaking a lens if a camera was aimed directly at him. Clea, however, might take a dim view of such behavior. It was time for him to leave.

But instead of a cameraman, Caroline peered around the pillar at him, her eyes the same intense green as her daughter's.

Wondering if she had any idea how close she'd come to triggering the violence and rage that simmered within him, Brand flexed his fists and forced a smile. "I seem to be causing something of a stir—I have to go. The last thing I want is to cause an incident. This is Clea's evening—it should be a wild success, not a brawl."

She nodded, and then whispered conspiratorially, "There are two journalists on the other side of the pillar— I'll stall them. Civility can be very hard to get away from. But, believe me, you and Clea always had something special. Whatever the problems, I'm sure you can get through them."

As Brand headed out, he wished he shared Caroline's confidence—and wondered if she'd noticed she'd finally called her daughter *Clea*.

Of course her bravado didn't last.

The sight of Brand leaving caused Clea's hard-won composure to flag. Faced by a flock of beaded and feathered designer ball gowns, ever-circulating trays of champagne and endless curious stares due to Brand's unexpected return, the last thing Clea wanted to do was party—even if it was to celebrate her success.

She wanted Brand back—the Brand she'd married, the husband she'd adored. To be held in his arms. To curl up against his body. Most of all, she wanted his assurance that he loved her, and that everything was going to be okay...

And she wanted to know where he'd gone...when she would see him again.

But duty called. So she plowed on, talking, laughing, saying all the right things. Refusing to reveal how shaken she'd been by the Brand she'd faced in her office: a dangerous, hard-eyed stranger. Or how her rock-solid confidence in what they'd once shared had been eroded.

An hour later, her father found her, his expression pugnaciously set in what she privately called his bulldog face, causing her inner tension to escalate. Helping herself to a glass of soda from a waiter's passing tray, Clea glanced surreptitiously over the rim of sparkling bubbles to her father's barreling approach. What she wouldn't give to be able to go home and crawl into the bed she'd once shared with the old Brand and examine every moment of the painful reunion with his frigid doppelgänger.

"That bastard's got gall showing up here after deserting you."

"Hush, Dad, let's not make a scene."

Donald tempered his voice. "The evening is over—people are leaving."

Clea glanced around. Plenty of onlookers still filled the museum. "So we can leave, too?" She tried to keep her voice light as she linked her arm through her father's.

In the foyer downstairs, the doorman saw them coming and picked up the handset to call her driver, Smythe, to bring the car around, while the cloak attendant retrieved her wrap. Clea smiled her thanks.

"Did he say where he's been?" her father asked as they exited through the glass doors.

There was no need to ask who he was referring to. Clea averted her face, not wanting her father—anyone—to read her confusion. She shook her head. "He wouldn't talk. He's angry about the baby."

"You told him about the baby?"

Clea picked her words with care. "I didn't have to. He guessed that I was pregnant."

"And he's far from pleased, I take it. What did you expect?"

Her father had tried to persuade her against having the baby, but Clea's mind had been made up.

"I told you it was a rash decision, that you shouldn't do it. But you wouldn't listen. Now it turns out your obduracy might just save the day."

"Dad…" Clea's voice trailed away. *Please, please don't let him say Brand shouldn't have come back.* She wouldn't be able to bear it. As much as the confrontation with Brand had shaken—shocked—her, the heady euphoria that he was actually alive still flickered under all the pain.

But her father was already saying, "You should not have married the man. It was a mistake. You should've married Harry—he's one of us."

One of us.

The thing her father had held against Brand all those years ago. *He's not like us.*

But from the moment Clea had encountered Brand at an auction, where he was inspecting the coins she'd been sent to bid on, she'd been fascinated. Still a student, her father had arranged a vacation job for her at the museum. She'd been briefed to bid on two Roman coins, and her enthusiasm had bubbled over. Until Brand told her that the coins were fakes—which was why there wasn't more interest in them.

Tall, handsome and with the kind of raw physical command she'd never encountered, Brand had intrigued Clea. His reasoning had been persuasive, his expertise obvious. In a quandary, Clea had first tried to call the assistant curator, then Alan Daley, and finally her father without any success.

So she'd made the decision not to bid.

Afterward, Brand had offered to buy her lunch but, knowing she had to get back to work and explain her decision, she'd declined. When he'd invited her to dinner instead, Clea had been overjoyed. By the end of the evening she'd been lost. She'd fallen in love with all the desperation of her nineteen-year-old heart.

Donald gave a deep sigh that broke into her reverie. "That man was trouble from the start."

"How can you say that?" The Lincoln was purring at the curb, but Clea made no move toward it. "Brand saved the museum from buying overpriced fakes the first day I met him."

"And had you in his bed within a week." Donald headed for the car.

It wouldn't be politic to admit that it had taken Brand far less time than that. Instead, Clea followed her father to the car and clambered into the backseat. Once inside, she said instead, "He married me a month later."

"A hasty affair that wasn't what you deserved."

"Dad, it was what I wanted." She wasn't in the right frame of mind to hear her father's favorite, much expounded opinion that Brand had only married her because she'd inherited a sizable sum of money from her maternal grandmother. "I can't cope with another lecture." Not tonight.

Tears pricked her eyes as Clea stared out the window, watching the city lights pass in a blur of color.

"Surely you're not going to cry over him?" Donald snapped. "The man deserted you, had an affair and got himself tangled up in God only knows what kind of mess in Iraq. You need to get rid of him."

His insensitivity caused her shoulders to stiffen. "I don't know that for sure."

"You saw photographs of a young beautiful woman who couldn't keep her hands off him." Her father gave a snort of disgust. "What more do you need? Fool yourself all you want, but at some stage you're going to have to face the truth."

A pang that could only be jealousy pierced her, adding to the turmoil of her emotions. "Dad, the same investigators also said that Brand had been killed in a crash and that locals had confirmed his body was thrown into a grave. They were clearly wrong about that, too." But now Brand himself had caused her doubts…

"Girl—" her father placed a hand awkwardly on hers "—I'm so sorry you have to face this, have to relive all the misery."

She brushed the tears from the corners of her eyes and sniffed. "These are happy tears—Brand's alive."

She tried to convince herself that was the truth. After the scene with Brand earlier, she suspected that a rocky road lay ahead.

Donald's hand tightened over hers and she could feel him studying her. "What was your mother doing at the museum?"

Clea's head whipped around. "She was there? I didn't see her."

"You didn't invite her?"

"No! I'd never do that without clearing it with you first."

The grim line of her father's mouth relaxed a little. "Good. I told her to leave."

Clea fought to ignore the funny feeling in her stomach caused by the news of her mother's dismissal. Then she steeled herself. She was no longer the ten-year-old girl her mother had abandoned for someone else's family.

She'd had enough. She'd had a long day, her feet ached from shoes that were too tight and her head spun from the emotional maelstrom she'd been through—the tussle about marriage with Harry, the shock of Brand's reappearance and her own inexplicable anger at him. She couldn't face discussing her mother, too.

Tomorrow it would be different. Better. Brand would've had a chance to get over his own shock. They'd talk. She'd explain why the baby was so important to her.

And he'd understand. Wouldn't he? She stared blindly out into the brightly lit night. For the first time the thought flitted through her mind that he might not.

Despite the warm evening Clea shivered, feeling more alone than since the night her mother had left.

Four

Brand strode into the Museum of Ancient Antiquities the following morning seething with frustration. He took the stairs two at a time. The glass doors guarding the management wing opened to him. No one manned the reception desk. So Brand continued along the corridor until through the glass wall of Clea's office, he could see her talking on the phone, doodling on a pad, her berry-red lips mouthing words he couldn't hear.

Suspicion, painful and ugly, shafted him. Was she talking to her lover? The father of her unborn child?

He studied her oblivious profile. Despite the sexy red lip color, he noted the absence of preening gestures and flirtatious mannerisms. Brand relaxed a little.

Not the lover then.

He pushed open the door. It made no sound, yet instantly her eyes tracked to him and tension filled the airy space.

"I have to go," she murmured into the handset. "Talk to you later, hon."

A girlfriend. No woman called her lover *hon*. His distrust appeased, Brand took his time surveying his wife's new office. Last night he'd been too preoccupied by Clea to take in the wall of bookshelves. At the foot of the shelves, open books were strewn over the woven carpet, revealing that Clea had been after information in a hurry. It was comforting to know that the inquiring, impulsive side of her still existed.

He crossed the room, passing a sleek, modern Le Corbusier chair on his way to the picture window. He looked down at the courtyard full of statues below. Visitors spilled out from the coffee shop onto the square, some perching on stone benches set around the edges of the paved concourse among bronze gods and goddesses.

"Very nice," he complimented her.

"Thank you. I've been here for three years, and I still appreciate it."

Three years. Not such a new promotion then. It highlighted how much of her life he'd missed. It had been around three years ago that his captors had gotten antsy. Vehicles had arrived at the camp in the dead of night, followed by huddled meetings. He'd heard the arguments, Akam's voice ringing out above the rest. A few nights later he'd been awakened and bundled into a car, a guard on either side, with Akam, as ringleader of the group, seated beside the driver, an AK-47 slung across his lap. The journey had been tense, but there'd been no checkpoints. No roadblocks. No glimpse of Coalition troops. The location of the new camp had been farther into the desert, the closest settlement an hour's drive away. In the days that followed, Akam's temper had been increasingly volatile, and Brand had known that any hope of escape, or rescue, had just grown slimmer. They'd moved camp regularly after that…but there had been one advantage—he'd only been locked up at night while the others slept. During the day he was allowed the freedom of the desert camps. It had saved his sanity.

"But I'm sure you didn't come to admire the view. What are you doing here, Brand?" Clea's voice interrupted the unpleasant memories of heat and dust and squalor.

Swiveling on his heel, Brand shoved his hands into the pockets of his denims. Clea had gotten to her feet and he watched through narrowed eyes as she advanced around the end of her desk.

"I stopped by my offices—or what were once my offices—this morning." Brand flexed his hands deep in his pockets. "There's a floor of accountants in the office space that used to be mine. Where is my PA? My staff?" He kept his tone even, determined not to show the wave of impotence that had swamped him after visiting the former site of his lucrative high-end antiquities dealership.

Clea stood still. "I'm sorry, Brand. I had to let your staff go. The business couldn't operate without your expertise."

His treacherous wife had been determined to eradicate all trace of him, Brand surmised.

Anger flared deep in his gut, masking the fear that had taken hold last night. At least anger he could control.

What he couldn't afford was to let her see his vulnerability…how raw and exposed he felt. He'd had years of practice in donning a mask of impenetrable reserve and showing no emotion, not even pain. Summoning that formidable control, Brand drew a slow breath and took his time to examine her. The fitted dress hugged her full breasts, the black linen rising and falling with every breath she took. He could've sworn her breathing quickened as he watched.

Sheer willpower stopped his eyes from sliding lower to the barely perceptible swell of her belly. The very thought of the pregnancy still left him reeling. Instead, Brand let his eyes linger on her red mouth, before lifting his gaze to meet hers.

Clea was frowning. "What do you want, Brand?"

He resisted the mad impulse that flouted fear and ached to say *you*—and settled instead for, "I also visited the bank."

The clerk hadn't even wanted to talk to Brand. To his shock, he'd been escorted to the door by security. In the past, bankers had fallen all over themselves to secure his business. Today's experience had been a rude awakening.

He faced Clea with the little information he'd gleaned from the clerk, his frustration bubbling over. "My accounts have been frozen. All of them. Apparently, *you* ordered it. So I assume the bank needs your authorization to activate them again." It burned Brand that he needed Clea to vouch for him.

She bent across the desk and flipped through a box holding business cards. Her black linen dress pulled tight across the shapely cheeks of her bottom.

The hot, heady rush of desire was unwanted. Brand swore silently, disconcerted to discover just how much his pregnant wife still turned him on.

"Ah, got it." Clea's fingers stilled as she found the card she was seeking. Pulling her diary across the desk, she flipped over the page and reached for the phone.

"What are you doing?" he demanded.

"Calling to make an appointment for us to go in to the bank tomorrow."

"Not tomorrow. Today," he insisted.

"I can't—"

Brand took a deliberate step forward, bringing him up

right behind her. "I want this resolved today. So clear your schedule."

Clea set the phone down. "Looming over me like this is not going to help. My to-do list is off the page. I simply can't do it today." She jabbed her finger at the diary on the desk. "The Museum Mile Festival is just over three weeks away."

The phone chose that moment to ring. With a mutter, Clea reached for it. Brand's hand closed over hers, preventing her from answering.

The ringing stopped abruptly. Her eyes darted to the caller-ID screen, then over her shoulder, to his face. "Brand, that's my boss!"

"Too bad."

She gave an impatient sigh. "Don't screw this up for me."

Clea had changed.

And he was only just beginning to realize how much. Despite the fact that she clearly hadn't spent the past few years waiting for him, Brand had still expected her to put him first. He'd been gone over four years. Secretly, he'd fantasized about not finding her at work today—and discovering her waiting for him at their home wearing nothing more than an inviting smile. It was rapidly becoming evident that he was no longer the center of her universe. But the ball of burning bitterness in the pit of his stomach wasn't going to bring back the Clea he'd spent every minute of four hellish years living for.

But crowding her, forcing her to acknowledge him, wasn't helping his cause.

So Brand rocked back on his heels and raised a mocking eyebrow, pushing harder, searching to find some sign that she still cared. "Since when has asking you for help become synonymous with screwing up?"

Strain showed in her eyes. "I'm more than happy to help you—I'll make the calls and take time out tomorrow. But if you're only here to play power games, then I'm afraid you'll have to leave. I've got stuff I need to check out for a brochure that's got to be at the printer's in a few hours." She gestured to the pile of books on the floor. "It can't wait."

There was an aching dignity about her, but Brand resisted the urge to pull her backward into his arms. Her refusal to instantly respond to his needs had placed him on the defensive. The old Clea would've put him first. "I'm checking out stuff, too. All the ways you've changed."

He took his time inspecting the length of her body available to his stare—the sweep of her back, the graceful curves of her hips, that gorgeous sexy bottom—and bit back a groan.

"Suit yourself." She glanced away, back down at the diary on her desk, so that—frustratingly—he couldn't see her face. "But it's not going to change the fact that I've got a job to do."

Brand followed her gaze down to the page she'd been doodling on when he'd entered her office. Hearts. She'd been drawing hearts. Perhaps she *had* been talking to her lover. He swallowed the bile at the back of his throat and inched forward until his jeans-clad thighs brushed her bottom. Somewhere in the recesses of his mind he knew he was being a jerk, but he couldn't help himself. Couldn't stop pushing to provoke a reaction, a burst of spontaneous emotion. The softness of her against his hip and thighs as he crowded closer caused his breath to catch.

And, God, her sweet scent—!

All at once adrenaline forked through him like lightning. Lowering his head, he murmured hoarsely against her nape, "Too busy for this?"

She twisted around and their eyes locked. Despite the sizzle in the air, hers were cool and distant. "Last night you said it was over."

The staccato words hit him in the solar plexus, knocking back his breath. Yes, he had said that. Stupid pride. Of course, he hadn't meant it. He'd been off balance. Hurting. Humiliated.

And betrayed...

How could he forget that? He was laying himself open for his heart to be ripped out again, for her to watch him bleed. To see his pain. *No way.*

Just in time, he slammed the mental door shut.

Clea shrugged out of his grasp. Penning a note in her diary, she said without looking at him, "If you don't mind, I'll make an appointment with the bank and confirm the time with you later."

He did mind.

And he was being dismissed. Disbelief shook Brand... and finally the fear surfaced. Fear that he'd irretrievably lost her. Fear that he would never find his way back into that laughter-filled, warm and comfortable world they'd shared together.

Fear that the past really was gone forever.

Then he took mental stock. Hell, what was he doing, yearning after a wife who'd found another lover? A lover by whom she was now pregnant.

Yet, before he could stop himself, Brand snagged her arm. Instantly, Clea spun around, her eyes wide with surprise. "What?"

Clea had accused him in the past of being too self-contained, never sharing his thoughts. Hell, how to explain that the thought of letting someone into the private space of his soul was terrifying? But this time he didn't spare himself—or her—as he pointedly studied her abdomen. "Was it an accident?"

Her breathing came in great rasps. Brand was conscious of the soft skin of her upper arm in his hold. Finally she croaked, "It wasn't an accident—I wanted this baby!"

The admission cut into his heart like a bayonet, causing every muscle to tighten until his whole body vibrated. "Why?"

"Not now, Brand."

"Yes, *now*."

The sound of voices drifted down the corridor outside Clea's office. She uttered a tense laugh. "This is ridiculous. You want to talk? You know, four years ago I thought the only thing wrong with our marriage was that you always kept your distance—you never talked to me about what you were thinking. Well, I was ready to talk last night... you weren't." Clea must have read something of his inner turmoil and tension in his face because she sighed. "We do need to talk, Brand. But not now. I've got work to do. Alan just called, he might come looking for me. Anyone could walk in on us."

"I don't care who walks in on us!"

"I do."

I do. She'd said those words to him during their wedding in the Chapel of Love—she'd vowed to love him, only him, forever. Brand brought his face close to hers. "I don't need the touchy-feely talk you consider so important. But I do want to know why you betrayed me, betrayed our vows."

Clea's chin came up. "*Betrayed* is a very strong word."

"That's what you did. Tell me why."

"It's not enough that you and I had dreamed of starting a family together?"

He snorted. "That's romantic hogwash."

"Hogwash?" Something flickered in her eyes. "Well,

then, this is going to sound like more touchy-feely romantic hogwash—I did it for the man I love."

"For your baby's father." It wasn't a question.

She nodded, her wide eyes suddenly wary. "Of course."

Even though he'd been expecting it, he was shaken by the confirmation that she'd betrayed him in the worst way possible—by falling in love with another man despite vowing to be his for the rest of their lives. The anger that had subsided when the fear arose spread like wildfire through his veins, heat leaping through him until Brand thought he might explode. He fought for cold control… and won.

Brand smiled at her, an easy, dismissive smile that nearly killed him. "And who is the lucky man?"

"You mean you haven't guessed?"

She studied him in a way that made him shift restlessly. He shrugged, and then lied through his teeth. "Frankly, I hadn't given it much thought."

"Oh." She glanced down at where his hand encircled her arm. "Let me go!"

At once Brand dropped her arm, walked away and leaned against the doorjamb, folding his arms across his chest with an insouciance he was far from feeling. The tension between them ratcheted up another notch.

When she looked up, the force of emotion in her expression rocked him back on his heels. So there was still…*something* under that composed exterior. It gave Brand the first surge of hope he'd experienced since walking into her office.

"I'm astonished that you haven't guessed," she said, flicking her hair back over her shoulders in the kind of go-to-hell gesture the Clea he'd married would never have used. It sorely tempted him to grab her and haul her into his arms. Kiss her into place. This new feistier Clea had the power to provoke him in a way no other woman ever had.

"So surprise me," he challenged instead of giving in to his baser impulses.

She glared at him, and he instantly itched to kiss her pursed lips. The memory of the sight that had met his eyes when he'd walked into the museum last night ignited him. As terrifying as any he'd witnessed in a war zone, it had kept him awake all last night in a dingy excuse for a hotel room with its peeling paint and water-stained ceiling.

Clea, his beautiful Clea, standing close to Hall-Lewis, her hand resting on his sleeve while he looked down at her. Bitterness, sharp and corrosive, burned at the back of Brand's throat.

"I don't need to guess." Hell, he'd known from the moment he touched her swollen stomach whose baby lay inside. "Harry Hall-Lewis."

Clea blinked twice. "You've never been dense, Brand. I should've known you'd work it out. Eventually."

Brand's conclusion that Harry was the father of her baby caused the sick churning in Clea's stomach to speed up.

She examined him where he leaned against the door frame, arms folded, ice-faced, blocking her escape. He looked nothing like the man she'd married. The long, dark waves of hair had been ruthlessly cropped to expose his strong jaw and the shuttered ocean-eyes. His mouth, always full and passionate, had flattened into a hard line.

The tightening in her stomach was the last thing Clea needed.

She told herself fiercely that she was not attracted to this hard, uncompromising Brand.

She couldn't be.

It would be stupid.

She had to get out of here.

Before she could have second thoughts, Clea surged past him and stalked out of her office through reception, retreating to the ladies' room down the hall, where she locked the door behind her. For once she failed to appreciate the beautiful antique mirror above the dark granite basin or the handcrafted brass sconces mounted on the walls. Instead, she turned on the faucet and let the cool water rush over her wrists, wishing the smoldering pain within her could be washed away so easily.

The glint of gold through the water trickling over her fingers gave her pause.

Slowly, Clea turned off the faucet. A second later her wedding ring was off. Bending her head so her curls fell forward, she stared at the plaited band of red, white and yellow gold resting in the palm of her right hand.

On their wedding day, Brand had told her that the red represented his passion, the white was for her, his bride, while the yellow represented the children they would have together…the family she'd always craved.

Her free hand touched her stomach, comforted by the presence of the life growing there. She would have the child they'd planned, but there would be no family…

Yet Clea had no regrets.

Making the decision to have the baby had filled the dark void in the days after she'd been forced to accept that Brand really was dead…or go mad. The memory of that conversation on their wedding day had become a lifeline, giving her a glimpse of a future where she would not be alone. She gazed at the ring. *Yellow for the children they would have.* Pursuing that dream was what had kept her sane.

For the life of her, Clea couldn't remember the to-do

list that only minutes ago had rumbled about in her head. She was overwhelmed by the aching loss of regret.

So much for hoping that today would bring perspective. So much for her intention of talking to Brand about the baby. It was proving to be impossible…

He'd changed too much.

Setting her wedding ring down on the cold granite slab, Clea picked a white towel off the waiting pile and wiped her damp hands before tossing the towel in a basket. Then she paused and critically inspected her reflection in the mirror. Green eyes set in a face framed by a riot of dark curls stared back at her. Nothing about her had changed. She looked the same as she had yesterday…last month… even last year. Certainly she didn't look nineteen weeks' pregnant.

Maybe a little slimmer, she finally admitted, and the sadness in her eyes hadn't been there four years ago.

Yet Brand had changed. While he'd always been self-contained and more than a little enigmatic, she'd never doubted that he loved her. But now he wasn't a little distant—he was on another planet. Whatever he'd have her believe, finding her pregnant could not possibly have been responsible for such a metamorphosis.

He no longer trusted her. No longer loved her. He believed she'd betrayed him and slept with Harry. If she'd—

Clea pulled herself up short.

No. She wasn't going to fall into the trap of blaming herself. This was *not* about her…or her pregnancy.

For reasons of his own, Brand had chosen to leave, to go to Athens without her four years ago, and then traveled on to Baghdad without letting her know, in the company of a woman with whom he'd once shared an intimate relationship.

His was not the behavior of a man committed to his marriage. It was time to face the fact that their marriage had been crumbling before he'd vanished—it was not the temple of strength built on the bedrock of love and trust that she'd believed.

"You did not drive Brand away," she told the Clea in the mirror. "So don't you dare blame yourself."

If she had to tell herself that ten times a day, a hundred times a day, she would do it. As long as it took for her to believe it. It had been Brand's choice to abandon her...and their marriage.

She glanced down to where the ring lay, the strands of gold warming the chill of the black granite. Already she missed the comfort of it on her finger.

Clea straightened her spine. Until Brand told her what had gone wrong, what had caused him to walk away from what they'd shared, she was not wearing his ring again.

Five

To Clea's immense relief, by the time she'd regained her composure sufficiently to emerge from the ladies' room, Brand had vacated her office. It took only a few minutes to call the bank and make an appointment for them with the manager the following day. But how to contact Brand to let him know?

Clea set the phone down and rose quickly to her feet. If she could catch him before he left the building…

She found him in the high-vaulted, airy west gallery, where he was examining the most valuable acquisition the museum had made since he'd vanished.

Summer sun spilled in through large, arched windows, illuminating Brand where he stood with his back to her, feet planted hip-width apart. It was impossible not to admire the way his jeans hugged his narrow hips or notice how the black T-shirt stretched across his powerful shoulders, and the sight caused a forbidden flutter beneath Clea's rib cage.

Brand's attention was focused on the two-foot-tall alabaster vase housed in a glass display cabinet equipped with state-of-the-art security sensors. Clea knew his features would reflect the same buzz of excitement that had gripped her the first time she'd seen the artifact. And still did even now, after six months of admiring the scenes carved in its two panels.

Yet he stood unmoving, not thrumming with excitement as she would have expected.

Clea hesitated.

Did Brand not know what he was looking at?

She dismissed the moment's doubt. *Of course he did.* This was Brand Noble, one of the world's up-and-coming experts on ancient artifacts…or at least he had been before he'd taken off without a word. She doubted his interest, or the sharp acumen he'd once possessed, had been dulled.

"What do you think?" Clea halted beside him. "Uruk period. Almost 3,500 years old. It's like having our very own Vase of Warka. Isn't it fabulous?"

"The Vase of Warka bore three panels of scenes of worship."

Clea rolled her eyes. "You know what I mean."

"There was a vessel very much like this in the Iraq Museum—I saw it once."

"I've heard that, too. The Vessel of Inanna," Clea said with a note of reverence in her voice. "But, unlike our treasure, that vase is in pristine condition, I believe. This piece has been substantially damaged—although it's been expertly repaired. Cost a king's ransom, let me tell you. Worth it, don't you think?"

His attention still on the vase, Brand said, "When I look at this vase I can't help but think of the theft of the Vase of Warka—completely different vase, nothing like this one, but stolen from the Iraq Museum during the sack of Baghdad."

"I know," Clea said with a touch of impatience.

"Of course, the story of the Vase of Warka had a sobering ending. Coincidentally enough, I was actually in Baghdad, part of a legion of troops stationed there, when it was returned two months later."

"You never told me that."

"It was surrendered under the watch of a group of surprised soldiers." Brand's voice was flat. Factual. "Thousands of years old, the Vase of Warka had been damaged, broken into fourteen pieces at some stage during the theft. An unnecessary price to pay for someone's greed."

Clea found herself bristling. "So why does our vase—" she pointed to the display case "—remind you of that incident?" She couldn't believe this conversation was heading where she suspected.

"You want me to spell it out?"

She wasn't going to let him draw her out like this. In the sunny voice she usually reserved for visitors to the museum and deep-pocketed moguls she was hitting up for funding, Clea said, "While it's true that the base of this vessel has been broken like the Vase of Warka's, I resent the implication that it was as a result of theft from the Iraq Museum. This is *not* the Vessel of Inanna that you saw there. This vase has sound provenance. I believe it was damaged a few years ago when the artifact was inspected for insurance purposes."

"And it wasn't mended then?" Brand's voice held disbelief.

"I found that strange, too," Clea admitted. "But the collector is aging, he found the maintenance taxing. We had it repaired shortly after acquiring it. You'll see that it wasn't the first damage. Eons ago it must've fallen because it has been mended by ancient craftsmen. See?"

Clea pointed to the giveaway restoration marks and slanted him a sideways glance, gauging his reaction. Not a flicker.

He turned his attention from the alabaster vessel and gave her a long look. "I do see, and I suspect it's highly likely it was stolen—and sold on the lucrative black market to a collector who would keep it behind heavily guarded doors."

Resenting the implication that she—or Alan Daley, the museum's aging head curator—would countenance black-market artifacts without provenance, Clea named their seller, a very well-regarded private collector. "And he acquired it in the 1960s—so it can't be the same vase that you saw."

One dark eyebrow shot up. "He willingly parted with what must be a crown jewel in his collection?"

Did Brand really have to make it sound as if there'd been foul play involved? Or was he just trying to wind her up? Keeping her tone dulcet, she responded, "He's an old friend of Dad's. He has no children…and his heirs have no interest in antiquities. And, as I said, the piece had been damaged. I think the poor man was thrilled that it would be repaired and displayed in the museum for countless people to see. We were very fortunate to be able to acquire some of his collection."

Brand's surprise was clear. "There are more pieces?"

"Oh, yes." Pride made Clea smile. "But they are still being catalogued—Alan checks out the provenance of every piece. But it helped that our collector is elderly and made most of his purchases before the 1970s. They won't be put on display for a while—the cleaning and restoration is taking vast amounts of time—although we will be unveiling one of the more spectacular pieces to coincide with the Museum Mile Festival."

The play of sunlight across his face did nothing to soften Brand's taut features.

Could he seriously be doubting the museum's professional integrity? Despite her efforts at calm, real annoyance finally started to stir. "And just to convince you of the care we took, Alan contacted the museum in Baghdad and confirmed that the Vessel of Inanna had not been looted. It's not on their inventory of missing artifacts."

Brand turned his head and their eyes locked. "I would've done exactly the same thing. But that doesn't guarantee it hasn't been looted, only that its disappearance hasn't yet been recorded."

The impact of those aqua eyes caused her next words to die unspoken on her lips. The connection between them was both fierce and primal. Her stomach bottoming out, Clea forgot about his suspicious reaction to the vase, his distrust of her. The color of his eyes became her whole world.

This was what it had been like from the very first moment they'd met.

No. Clea blinked, breaking the spell, and drew a shivery breath. Pushing a hand through her hair, she brushed it away from her overheated face.

She didn't want this...this...

Brand's gaze sharpened and he caught her hand. As his thumb brushed the pale indent where her wedding ring had sat, sensation bolted through her.

"You're not wearing your wedding band."

"I took it off."

Something flashed behind those marvelous eyes, an emotion that made her heart tighten.

"Why?"

From outside the gallery, Clea heard the rising chatter of voices and her eyes flicked to the open double doors on the far side of the room. One of the volunteer tour guides was shepherding a group of tourists into the gallery. Clea caught a word or two of Japanese.

Grateful for the respite, she said, "Look, this isn't the place for this discussion."

Brand didn't move, he only repeated, more insistently, *"Why?"*

Clea shot a harried glance to the doorway. Several of the tourists were staring curiously. Clea could just imagine the picture she and Brand presented. A man and a woman, standing so close together, his hand holding hers, the charged air between them...electric.

Her cheeks grew hotter. "We're making a spectacle of ourselves."

Without waiting for Brand's agreement, she tugged her hand free of his grasp and rushed out of the gallery as though the devil himself was on her heels.

Brand filled the doorway of her office, a dark and brooding presence.

Perhaps the devil himself had indeed arrived...

Clea shook off the image and drew a deep breath. Her reaction to Brand's stare, the touch of his hand on her ring finger, had shaken her. The attraction he'd always held for her appeared to be as strong as ever...even though he hated her.

What was wrong with her?

He'd deserted her for another woman. How could she even be tempted by a man whose contempt for her was palpable? *Insanity.* But there was a way out. A way that would put him forever out of her reach.

Could she do it? Could she burn her bridges forever? Clea drew a shuddering breath. Then she reminded herself that he hadn't been prepared to listen when *she* had wanted to talk. Nor had he been prepared to offer explanations when she'd all but begged for them.

Brand no longer loved her. Suspicion. Distrust. *Hatred.* That was what he felt for her.

Now she had to think about self-preservation.

The time for damage control was long past. Now she had to look out for herself...for her baby. What did his opinion of her matter? It could hardly get any worse. She'd use every means at her disposal to build a wall around her susceptible heart, to construct a citadel Brand couldn't breach.

Clea refused to let her vulnerability to Brand sabotage her life. Not when she'd struggled to rebuild something from the wasteland his disappearance had created...

"I took the ring off because—" She broke off and swallowed. Something nagged at the back of her mind. She pushed the uneasy sensation away, and focused on Brand. Their marvelous marriage had been nothing more than a mirage. She was entitled to salvage her pride— to save face. "Last night was more than the exhibition opening."

Brand had gone still and narrow-eyed. Sun rays caught his cheekbones, highlighting the hard angles but failing to disperse the shadows that occupied the deep grooves bracketing his mouth. He certainly looked as frightening as the devil. Clea shivered. No love there. Only darkness.

"Harry asked me to marry him and—"

"No!" The sound exploded from him.

She warded him off with outstretched hands—even

though he hadn't moved from where he appeared to have taken root in the woven carpet. In a rush, she added, "And I said yes." Clea raised her chin and her eyes clashed with Brand's. "A child needs a father."

Silently, she apologized to Harry for her cowardice. But it would be easier this way. Brand had already concluded that the baby was Harry's. And she didn't want him back... not this cold-eyed, suspicious stranger who didn't love her enough to trust her. She certainly wasn't going to allow him to seduce her traitorous body.

"You can't marry Hall-Lewis...you're married to me."

"No, I'm not. You're dead."

"Excuse me?" Brand padded closer, big and suddenly looking extremely dangerous. "I'm very much alive."

Clea edged toward the door as his bulk blocked out the sun. "Not legally—I had you declared dead."

"What?"

"You're dead, Brand. As far as everyone else is concerned, I'm a widow."

Brand's mouth twisted. "That's a load of bull. I'm here...alive...and you're still my wife."

He paused, and Clea saw him make the connection.

"Declared dead," he said softly. "So that's why my accounts were frozen."

The look in his eyes made her feel sick. "Yes, until your estate is finalized. Then your assets will be distributed." She'd forgotten to tell him about the appointment she'd made for the bank in the morning. "Brand—"

"And you, of course, inherit it all."

Clea didn't like the bleak expression that dulled his eyes.

"Now I understand your motivation for having me declared dead."

"Brand, I don't need your money. I have my inheritance, I have a job—"

"That Daddy arranged for you," he sneered.

Clea felt the blood drain from her face. His jibe was unforgivable. "I've never cared about money. My father's connections might have gotten me an introduction to the museum, but I got my job—and every promotion after that—based on merit. I'm responsible for my own success. You can't take that away from me." Clea brushed back her corkscrew bangs with her hand, and then dropped the ringless hand out of sight when Brand's jaw locked. "I've made an appointment with the bank for tomorrow morning."

"Better call the lawyers and have that court order declaring me dead rescinded, too," he growled.

Clea nodded, then swallowed as the tension that had been simmering between them took on a pulsing life of its own. The sudden silence only heightened her consciousness of every move Brand made, of the way his chest expanded under the black T-shirt so that he seemed to loom closer with every breath.

She took a small step toward the door.

But Brand got there first.

He closed in until she came up against the smooth glass of the door. *Trapped.* Clea froze as he bent forward.

His familiar scent surrounded her; she inhaled the essence of him, and her knees went weak.

From this close she could see the smooth line of his jaw where he'd shaved. His lips parted, the full bottom one reminding her of the pleasure that mouth had given her in the past.

Tiny shivers prickled up her spine, spread across her nape and down her arms, bringing an urgent electric awareness she truly didn't need.

He leaned in farther, a dark hulk of shadow, and her heart skipped a beat…make that three.

Brand was going to kiss her.

She stopped breathing. Self-preservation was drowned out by a stronger emotion.

Brand whispered her name, softly, a gentle hiss across her skin. She suppressed the flurry of quivers. An ache unfurled low in her belly. Without thought, she moistened her lips.

Brand exhaled, a sharp burst of sound.

Clea's muscles clenched. She could already feel his mouth…taste him…

The last time she'd experienced this breathless nervousness had been in the over-the-top Chapel of Love in Las Vegas. But while there'd been the same sense then of being poised on the edge of a precipice, about to step into a whole new world, it had been different. There'd been anticipation. Hope. And happiness. They'd been in love, there'd been none of this knife-edge tension.

Back then Clea had known that fleeing to Vegas to marry Brand would mean trouble, but she'd been confident that her father would quickly forgive her—despite his reservations about Brand. She'd been eager to avoid her father's objections, the obligatory big, white wedding bash, full of guests she barely knew. Sure, Vegas had been neither special nor intimate, but her heart had been set on Brand. She loved him, after all.

He was her forever. From that first fateful moment at the auction when he'd cautioned her against bidding on the fake Roman coins.

Now Brand's thumb came down on the moist swell of her lower lip. His touch was surprisingly rough against her slickness. Her tongue probed his skin. He tasted of salt and musk. Of aroused male.

The old, never-forgotten thud of her heart began, and Clea melted. This time she licked his thumb with slow deliberation. Her tongue swirled into the tender fold that separated his thumb from his forefinger.

They had a second chance.

It was going to be okay...they could work it out.

His mouth came down on hers, and Clea's lashes fluttered lower. The glass was hard and cool behind her; by contrast, Brand's passion was hot. He shifted, and a moan broke from her throat. The kiss deepened. Her hands crept up his T-shirt, caressing the back of his neck.

The pressure of his mouth ceased abruptly.

Clea opened her eyes.

Brand moved back, putting an arm's-length distance between them, his eyes horribly knowing. "Well, I'd better go—you've been telling me you've got so much work to do, and I'm keeping you from it. And on second thought, I'll instruct my lawyers to have the order presuming my death set aside. That way I won't be using up your valuable time."

Bastard...

So he knew she wanted him. How humiliating. He was going to leave her hanging like this...ravenous for him. She clenched her hands, determined not to reach for him, restrain him, beg him to kiss her...just once more.

How easily he'd demolished the barriers she'd tried to erect against him. How easily she'd forgotten about Anita...

She heard him move, and caught the scent she would always recognize as Brand's as he advanced again. "Take this as a warning," he growled in her ear.

Refusing to cower, she glared at the broad bulk of his chest, the muscle clearly defined beneath the snug fit of the black T-shirt.

Brand placed his fingertip under her chin, and tipped it up, forcing her to meet his eyes.

"I'm far from dead." He gave her a dangerous stare that caused her stomach to flip. "And while you might be planning to marry another man, you still want *me*. Think about that—because I intend to think of nothing else…all night long."

Without giving her a chance to respond, he released her chin, turned and sauntered away.

Biting her lip ferociously to quell the frustrated sob that threatened, Clea watched him leave. And, even though everything in her screamed not to let him walk through the door, her limbs had turned to Jell-O. She heard the door whisper shut and through the glass she watched until he turned the corner and disappeared from her line of sight. His footsteps faded.

There was only silence.

Her shoulders slumped. Too drained to move, she tipped her head back against the coolness of glass, and fervently wished she never had to see Brand Noble again.

Arrogant bastard. He didn't deserve her loyalty!

Well, she had no way of even contacting him—she'd have to wait for him to reach out to her. If he ever did.

At least she'd taken the first step toward weaning herself off the intensity of her feelings for Brand. She'd taken off his ring…and he knew it.

The nagging unease from earlier returned in full force.

His ring.

Clea started. *Her ring.*

Oh, no! Adrenaline shocked through her as she stumbled out her of office. She could still visualize where she'd set it down on the granite counter top. She'd dried her hands, but afterward she'd failed to pick the ring up.

By the time she yanked open the door to the ladies'

room, her pulse was pounding. Dread mushroomed as her gaze fell on the granite slab beside the hand basin.

Her ring was gone.

<u>Six</u>

Brand shouldered his way through the summer crowds on Fifth Avenue.

Overhead, skyscrapers cut the blue sky into jigsaw shapes. Brand had thought he'd long ago hit rock-bottom. Clea had proved him wrong. The past hour had shaken his life to its very foundations.

On the corner he hailed a cab and gave an address, his stony face preventing the cabdriver from launching into conversation. When the cabbie ferociously gunned the accelerator, Brand's face didn't relax into a smile.

Not even the puzzle presented by the museum's newest exhibit could keep his mind off Clea's latest revelations. She'd taken off her ring. She'd agreed to marry Hall-Lewis.

And she'd already had him declared dead.

While he'd been thinking about her every day, consumed by how to find his way back home to her, she'd been planning how to bury him alive.

"Can't you drive faster?"

The cabdriver obliged. Brand stared blindly out the window as the city flashed past. In his old life he'd been impatient. Maybe too impatient. But his captivity—where minutes had stretched into hours and hours into days—had changed that. He'd acquired the ability to block out everything except what he most wanted: to survive.

The cab stopped outside a brownstone in a tree-lined avenue. Brand paid the cabbie with the last of the dollars Akam had lent him and headed for the house he'd bought for Clea back in what seemed like another lifetime. On the front door, brass letters spelled out Welcome Home.

Brand pressed the buzzer.

He didn't recognize the short, bald manservant who opened the front door. "Where is Bright?" Brand demanded, surprised not to see the elegant, stooped man he and Clea had hired in happier times.

"Bright retired last year, s—"

The butler ran his assessing gaze over Brand's no-label jeans and the black T-shirt that hugged his muscled torso and biceps before biting back the rest of the automatically polite *sir*. Having priced and dismissed Brand's clothing, he stated, "We're not employing bodyguards."

Brand gave the stranger barring the way into his home a lethal glare. "I'm not looking for a job. I'm Brandon Noble."

The butler stood firm, his solid body filling the doorway, disbelief glittering in his eyes. "Mr. Noble is dead."

Was he never going to escape that myth?

While the butler's pugnacious attitude rankled, the man was only doing his job. Brand finally took pity on him and extracted a passport so new the dark cover was still stiff.

He flipped it open and flashed the identification page at the man. "Satisfied?"

The butler glanced at the photo taken less than a week ago in the back room of Akam's cousin's house and then back to Brand. His throat worked and he said thinly, "It appears I must apologize, Mr. Noble."

With mordant humor, Brand suspected the butler was torn between evicting a possible interloper and risking his job if Brand's claim proved to be true. Just as well the man wasn't versed in detecting excellently crafted fakes.

"No apology necessary." Brand pocketed the fraudulent passport and raised an eyebrow. "I didn't catch your name."

Both of them knew the butler hadn't supplied it.

Discomfort crossed the butler's face. "My name is Curtis. The doctor is still at the museum, sir."

The doctor.

The butler was referring to Clea. That was another piece of information she'd neglected to share with him—she'd gotten her PhD. Graduated. Something else he'd missed out on. He ought to have been beside her, celebrating her success. Brand tamped down his frustration at the tragic unfairness of it all. If he allowed resentment and anger to bubble over, he'd go mad.

"I know she is," he said calmly. "I've just come from there."

Relief relaxed the butler's frown. "Then you'll come back when the doctor is home?"

To prevent a pointless standoff, Brand asked, "Is Smythe still on the staff?"

It galled him to have to ask a man he didn't know if the chauffeur still worked for him. One day he'd been in control of every element of his life, and the following day he hadn't known where the next meal was coming from, even if it would come at all…or what his fate would be.

Death. Or life.

For four years the balance had hung in the hands of his captors.

The butler nodded, but he still blocked the doorway. Brand stepped forward. "Find him, Curtis," he snapped. "I'm not standing here all day."

Five minutes later Brand was inside his own home.

A smiling Smythe stood nearby, tears streaming down his wrinkled cheeks as Brand, his own throat thick with emotion, scanned the inside of the home he hadn't seen for years.

Home. Yet not home.

It was subtly different. Stark white walls had given way to shadowy hues that formed an admirable backdrop for the Kandinsky he and Clea had bid for in an auction a month after they'd bought this house. The large ship's chest that had once stood against the wall had been replaced with a walnut sideboard, giving the hallway an unfamiliarity he hadn't foreseen.

Brand shrugged off the sense of dislocation. Clea had changed beyond recognition—new man, new baby, new life—so why the hell should the house have remained the same?

He took the carpeted stairs two at a time and, at the end of a passage lined on one side with high-arched windows, strode into the master bedroom.

The curtains were new—a botanical print that added a light, green note to the sumptuous richness of the ivory wallpaper. His gaze moved on, seeking out familiar signs of Clea's daily life. Except for a vase that held tall white blooms and two crystal scent flagons, the dressing table was empty of feminine clutter.

Secret notes of jasmine lingered in the air.

Afternoon sunlight filtered through the spreading

branches of the chestnut outside the window, dappling the pristine bedcover. The magnificent mahogany sleigh bed he and Clea had chosen together after spending a hilarious Valentine's Day trying out beds what seemed like a century ago still gave the room warmth and contrasted with crisp white linen.

He'd made love to his wife on this bed more times than he cared to remember. Here they'd shared dreams. Promises. And passion…

The plush carpet muffled his footsteps. Brand halted in front of wide windows and looked through the boughs of the chestnut tree, across the backyard to a glade of silver birches, the warmth of the summer evening on his face. Nothing like the scorching desert heat of the Middle East.

Unbidden, he remembered that charged moment in Clea's office, the heat of her tongue as he'd touched her lip… God, he'd been tempted never to stop, to pull her to him in a bone-crushing hold and bury himself intimately in her softness.

But he'd been too angry. Here, in this bedroom where they'd shared so many hours of happiness, it might be different.

This was home.

And Clea was his wife—not his widow.

Placing flat palms on the wide, white-painted windowsill, Brand leaned forward and breathed in the perfumed mix of jasmine and gardenia from the garden below.

A snapshot of the past flashed back to him. The kind that had steeled him through his darkest days, strengthening his determination to return to Clea, yet now bringing only immeasurable pain.

The first time they'd discussed having children had been on a glorious summer day like today, the kind that only New York could provide, with washed blue skies, golden sunlight and the slightest ripple of a breeze. Clea had prepared a picnic basket and together they'd ventured down to Central Park.

"Four boys," she'd declared, leaning back on her elbows on the newly mown grass after she'd wiped the last crumbs of delicious apple pie from her lips.

"What?" The shock of her demand had forced his attention from her mouth to her eyes, hoping to find that she was joking. She wasn't. The green eyes had held a dreamy glow. Leaning back against the scarred trunk of an oak, Brand had echoed, "*Four* children?"

"Make that five. All boys. I want a big family."

"Five boys?" he sputtered. "It's not all roses."

He should know. Brand was one of four brothers, and he knew Clea envied him that.

"I don't care," she said, her mouth tilting into a smile. "I hated being an only child. You're lucky! I wish *I* had siblings."

"You can have mine anytime you want."

"Okay, I'll take you up on that. But I wish your brothers lived closer—I wish we could visit often, be a family."

Two of his brothers still lived in New Zealand, while the youngest was in London. Brand kept in touch with them, with a careless affection that drove Clea crazy.

"You aren't wriggling out of this, Brand. Five children. Absolute minimum."

He'd pushed away from the rough bark of the oak and dropped down onto the grass beside her. "I'm happy to oblige, but we'd better get busy—five boys are going to take some work." And he'd kissed her squarely on her open mouth.

That had been the end of any talk of children for a while.

Now, leaning on the windowsill of their bedroom, Brand stared at the weepy boughs of the birches at the end of the yard, barely noticing how much they'd grown in his absence. Clea was pregnant. But not with his child. It was not their dream that she was fulfilling. It was Clea's new dream—part of her vision of a future with Hall-Lewis.

Surrounded by the rich warmth of their bedroom, Brand knew he had to fight for his own future with Clea. The next stop would be a visit to his lawyer, who would no doubt be stunned to see him. His legal eagle could finally earn the handsome retainer Brand had always paid, by resurrecting him from the dead. Legally.

His and Clea's marriage was far from over.

It was a marriage that had been cracked wide open to its foundations. Distrust. Betrayal. Brand's breath hissed out as he straightened up. Across the garden, the silvery leaves of the birches quivered in the summer breeze. But there would be no divorce. He might not be the father of her unborn child, yet, despite everything, Clea was still his wife. For better or worse.

Not Hall-Lewis's bride.

It might not be the family they'd planned together, but the baby existed. *Another man's baby.* Brand shoved his hands into his jeans' pockets. He would learn to live with it. Far easier than the alternative of living without Clea.

With that decision made, the monstrous tension within him started to ease.

He was not going to let Hall-Lewis take her away from him without a fight.

He was home to stay.

Clea let herself into the darkened house.

Sconces cast soft shadows in the corners of the hall,

and her heels tapped across the dark wooden boards as she walked toward the carpeted stairs.

Upstairs, Curtis had already turned off the overhead lights, leaving only a muted glow from a lamp on the sideboard to light her way.

At the end of the passage the bedroom door was open a crack. Clea knew the bedcovers would already be turned down. Pushing the door wide, Clea made for the dim silhouette of the bed and sat down on the edge. After slipping her high-heeled pumps off, she leaned forward and flicked on the bedside light.

Rising to her feet, she eased the zipper of her black linen dress down and wiggled the straps over her shoulders.

"A striptease wasn't quite what I had in mind, but don't let that stop you."

Clea whirled around, clutching the bodice of the dress to her breasts, and stared at the man who lay in the king-size bed, his arms folded behind his head, watching her through narrow, inscrutable slits.

"You nearly gave me a heart attack. What are you doing here?" she demanded, her heart still thudding with fright. "In my house?"

"Waiting for you." Brand arched a dark eyebrow in a way that caused her stomach to flip.

The first thing that struck Clea was that—despite his air of lazy arrogance—Brand was angry. The second was that his shoulders and chest were bare.

"You're not wearing any clothes!"

His mouth curled. "You also forgot that I sleep naked?"

Naked. It conjured up visions that made her sweat. Clea found herself flushing. She'd seen Brand naked a million times. They'd made love. Passionate love. So why did that one little word now cause her to shiver like a virgin?

Brand was smiling, a tiger-got-the-cream kind of smile

that caused Clea to suspect he knew exactly how the word *naked* made her squirm inside. No doubt he'd said it to provoke precisely this response. What had he said earlier? *And while you might be marrying another man, you still clearly want me. Think about that—because I intend to think of nothing else...all night long.*

No. Clea tightened her grip on the dress hugged against her breasts, making sure it didn't slip. "Get out of my bed," she said in a rush. Whatever Brand had in mind, she wasn't about to fall into bed with him like an overripe, ready-to-be-devoured peach.

"Our bed." The disconcerting gleam in his eyes warned her that he knew she was rattled. While she flushed, he murmured in a husky, suggestive undertone, "Don't tell me your fiancé wears pajamas?"

About to heatedly deny that she had a fiancé, Clea remembered in the nick of time that she'd told Brand she was marrying Harry and bit back the retort. She'd never been much good at deception. But revealing that she'd lied would only leave her more exposed. He'd demand to know why. Clea cringed as her discomfort grew. And she had no intention of letting him glimpse the hole he'd ripped in her heart.

At least the fiancé fiction gave her some protection from the unwanted effect Brand's physical presence had on her. Letting Brand believe she was marrying Harry salvaged her pride, and gave her the chance to think through how she was going to deal with Brand's betrayal. Even though on the inside she was a mass of tremors.

Fiercely determined not to reveal her vulnerability to him, she tossed her head back and countered, "Didn't you consider that by coming here tonight you might've bumped into him?"

"I considered it." Brand's eyes flared to a shade of pure,

bright turquoise. "To be honest, I was looking forward to the encounter."

Clea did a double take at the dangerous glint in his eyes. This was the dark side of Brand she'd known must exist, but had never seen. It frightened her. Brand had served in the SAS; he possessed skills—knowledge—she'd never wanted to know about. He could take Harry apart.

Had she made a terrible tactical mistake telling Brand she was going to marry Harry? Had she put Harry in danger? Clea gulped down a breath of air, and told herself that she was overreacting. Brand's self-control was phenomenal—he would never hurt Harry. Already the glint in his eyes had changed to a more familiar gleam that had her exhaling in a rush of relief.

This Brand she could deal with.

He lifted the edge of the covers invitingly. "But your fiancé is not here, and you're already halfway to naked. Drop that dress. Come, get in."

Her heart skipped a beat. Her crushing inability to resist him was the whole reason for the lie she'd told. "Not a chance."

His lips curved into a lethal smile. "Am I supposed to come get you?"

Clea shivered at the blatant promise in his eyes. He would do it. And he was naked under that sheet…

Get out now.

"You're utterly impossible!" Yanking the dress higher over her breasts, she flounced across the room before temptation could undo her. "This has gone far enough. I'm going to take a shower, and when I come out I want you out of here. You can choose any of the guest bedrooms, but this is my room."

As she slammed the door to the master bathroom

she heard him growl, "And this is *my* bed. You are *my* wife—even though that's something else you appear to have forgotten."

Seven

Not even the sting of the shower jets could banish the outrage that gripped Clea. Yet beneath her fury lurked the knowledge that she'd escaped into the bathroom to avoid the sight of Brand climbing out of her bed in all his naked glory. Much easier to focus on her angry confusion.

How dare Brand walk into *her* home, climb into *her* bed, lean up against *her* pillows, taking over her most intimate sanctuary as if it had been only yesterday that he'd vacated it? And then have the brazen *gall* to remind her that she was still his wife?

She wasn't the one who had left!

Clea turned her face up to the battering spray. The man propped up on her pillows in the room next door was a world away from the man she'd married, the man who'd pledged to love her until death did them part.

This man despised her.

This man had walked away from the vows they'd taken.

Turning off the water, she squeezed gel into her trembling hand and spread it along her arms. The action soothed her. Clea stroked the creamy lather over the ripe curves of her breasts that had become increasingly tender as her pregnancy had progressed, and, drifting down, she gently rubbed the newly discernible swell filling the hollow that had, until recently, stretched between her hips.

A secret fluttering—like the whisper of invisible butterfly wings—caused her hands to still. The thrilling sensation had started two weeks ago.

Her baby was moving.

A baby who had been created to seed the family she and Brand had once dreamed of growing together in another lifetime. A time in which she'd been certain of his love.

They'd been married four weeks after meeting— and he'd vanished ten months later. A stranger who had intimately shared her life—her love—for less than a year. One she'd prayed for and believed in for all the years he'd been gone. But had she really known Brand at all? Had he ever loved her in the way she'd believed?

The confusion shifted again—like a kaleidoscope— offering a different vision. *Was* Brand's leaving her fault? Had she loved him too much, stifled him with her desperation for a family? Clea shut her eyes. Water beat against her face, her breasts, her belly. Clea shivered. Opening her eyes, she attacked the faucets, turning up the heat. A welcome blast of hot water sluiced over her, drowning out her unspoken terror.

She couldn't bear to consider the possibility that she'd driven him away, as she'd once driven her mother away... into the arms of another man's family.

Had she done the same thing to Brand? Or had his bond to Anita been too strong to break? And, if that was the case, why had he finally come home?

Too many questions whirled through Clea's head. But, one thing was certain: She wasn't sharing a bed with Brand. Not tonight. Not until she had answers.

Maybe never.

The water in the bathroom had stopped running.

Brand watched the door, every muscle tense, waiting for it to open.

At last Clea emerged, a shadowy wraith draped in an all-covering bath sheet. The pale skin of her shoulders glistened with moisture. He quickly shut his eyes. The soft press of her bare feet against the carpet told him she was approaching the bed.

Brand waited, giving her time.

She paused for a long, simmering moment beside the bed. Then she said, "Brand? Are you asleep?"

He didn't answer, and concentrated on keeping his breathing slow and regular. He'd had plenty of practice over the past few years—perfecting the technique to fool even the most sharp-eyed guards.

Clea sighed sharply. "You can't sleep here."

Despite her annoyance, Brand had no intention of sleeping anywhere else. This was *his* bed...and she was *his* wife. She'd eventually come to terms with the fact that he wasn't moving out. The sooner she got over her fit of pique, the better for both of them.

"Wake up."

She touched his shoulder, her fingers surprisingly gentle and slightly damp from her shower. Brand forced himself not to react and kept his breathing shallow.

"You're too heavy for me to move. I suppose you banked on that." The bed shifted as she sank down on the edge. "I should call Curtis to help me move you. It would serve you right if the whole household knew I'd kicked you out of my bedroom."

His eyes opened a tiny crack.

She sat with her back to him, her hair spilling over her shoulders, tempting him to touch it. Clea couldn't be serious about calling the staff to kick him out. It would provide fodder for the kind of scurrilous gossip she'd always scrupulously avoided. Nor could he imagine the old Clea rousing the chauffeur who'd already gone to bed for the night.

In the dim glow of the bedside lamp he could see that her head was bent, and her shoulders sagged. She looked weary, and curiously defeated.

Brand ached to lift the covers, strip the damp towel away from her body, and sweep her into the warm comfort of the space beside him. But then she'd know he was awake—and they'd be trapped back in the spiraling turbulence between them. So he resisted the impulse and continued to squint through almost-closed lids.

He was going to win this round. Clea had no choice but to get into bed beside him—she would realize that soon enough. Anticipation seeped through him.

"What are you doing here? Why are you back, Brand?"

God help him, he no longer knew. For years his only goal had been to get back to Clea. He'd never given up on his determination to come home. Since the episode last year when a messenger had arrived with news that made Akam rage with fear, and had led to Brand being severely beaten, Brand had known his kidnappers were at the breaking point. By feeding Akam's growing paranoia, Brand had secured his own release. His kidnapper had provided transport to the north. Armed with a crudely drawn map, Brand had headed into the mountains in search of a network of Kurdish smugglers Akam had told him about. Three days' backbreaking walk under the scorching sun had gotten him to the village they inhabited. From there he'd had help—and setbacks that had wasted more months—before making it through the smugglers' pass in the mountains. Once in Turkey, he'd been provided with two fake passports—one in his own name and another identity to travel on—before starting the long haul home to America.

Akam's Turkish cousin Ahmet had warned him not to use the passport in his own name in case it set off alarms in some government agency. Yet even though it was a fake, having a passport in his own name reassured him that Brand Noble still existed.

He'd expected—

Brand shut his eyes tighter. What the hell did it matter what he'd expected? He'd arrived home ready to embrace his old life…only to find Clea denying his existence. He'd gotten back to a wife who was pregnant…and planning to marry another man.

Unless he convinced her otherwise.

Clea bent toward him. For a heart-jolting second he thought she was going to hug him—kiss him even. That moment earlier when she'd realized he was naked beneath the covers—when her eyes had stretched wide with shock…awakening want—still tantalized him. For an instant he forgot to keep his breathing even; it came in jagged bursts.

But Clea didn't notice. Her hands were too busy searching beneath the pillow.

Brand lost patience. He wanted his wife back. Giving a groan, he rolled toward her. Still pretending to be deep in a stupor, he flung an arm across her back and pulled.

She leaped back and his arm fell away. Through almost-shut eyes he caught a glimpse of a length of jade silk and lace crumpled between her hands. Brand rolled away.

Behind him Clea muttered, "That's it. I'm going to sleep in the nursery, and you can go to hell!"

With a decisive click of the bedside lamp switch, Clea plunged the room into darkness. Brand listened to her feet padding softly across the carpet, then the bedroom door banged shut.

Brand winced and opened his eyes wide against the overpowering dark.

Damn.

This wasn't the outcome he'd planned when he'd moved back into the house today.

Rolling onto his back, he stared into the darkness. It was going to be a long night.

Clea didn't know it, but he didn't need to be sent to hell—he'd already been there. It had turned out to be a hot, lonely place where sleep dried up and dreams died.

Even the hardiest hope struggled to survive.

It was only the strength of his desire to come home to Clea that kept him fighting. Against all odds, he was free; he'd succeeded.

Only to find himself in a hell worse than the one he'd left behind.

Despite his lack of sleep, it didn't take Brand long to work out why Clea had changed banks for her own accounts.

Ted Walters, the banker who had refused to take his calls, wore a black suit, frameless glasses and an air of arrogance that caused Brand to grit his teeth. Degrees in gilt-edged frames hung on the wall behind where Walters posed in a black-leather executive chair. Sliding a glance to where Clea sat beside him, Brand tried to gauge whether she was experiencing the same irritation with the banker's self-importance. In a jade silk dress, with her hands folded in her lap, she looked cool and utterly composed.

Brand transferred his attention back to Walters.

"Your accounts were frozen on Mrs. Noble's instruction," Walters told him in a smug voice from behind the relative safety of four feet of polished wood. "Until your estate is finalized we can't pay anything out. So I'm sorry—we are not in a position to advance you any funds." He didn't sound apologetic at all.

Brand allowed his mouth to curl. "You appear to have missed the crux of the matter—my estate will not be finalized. I'm very much alive."

Walters started to frown, then drew a sheet of paper from the file in front of him. "This is a copy of the court order having you pronounced dead. I'm afraid we can't do anything until that is overruled."

The situation was absurd. Brand might have laughed, if he wasn't so sure the banker was gaining some kind of perverse pleasure from this.

Clea leaned forward. "But Brand is here. Surely if he provides you with proof of identity—"

Brand shook his head. His driver's license had long since disappeared, and the passport he carried was a forgery. He certainly had no intention of producing it for the banker's inspection. Until those documents were replaced, all he possessed was the birth certificate that Clea had retrieved from the document safe in their bedroom. "That won't be necessary. My lawyers will have that order set aside by noon." Brand glanced at his watch to underscore the point he was making—it was almost noon now.

Refocusing his attention on Walters, he gestured to the copy of the presumption of death order, and said softly, "Since that obstacle will be removed very shortly, you may as well begin unfreezing my accounts. I have considerable assets—some of my investments should have matured very nicely while I've been gone—and I will be taking charge of them."

"Well, we certainly look forward to doing business with you in the future." Walters extracted a business card from a brass holder beside an ornate pen stand and offered it to Brand. "We would, of course, hope you will persuade Mrs. Noble to reconsider the decision she made while you were…away…to move her accounts."

He made Clea sound like some malleable little airhead who did precisely as her husband ordered. Brand shot his wife a quick glance. Her green eyes had turned stormy. For the first time in a long while, Brand fought the urge to smile with genuine amusement. Walters did not know his wife.

Ignoring the banker's card, he said, "I certainly wouldn't consider telling Dr. Noble what to do." Brand made sure the emphasis on Clea's qualification would not been missed. "My wife is intelligent—and informed—enough to make her own decisions. Keeping my own business here would, of course, require that you were no longer handling my account—the level of service has been sadly lacking."

The banker started to look concerned. "But—"

Brand cut him off. "The service will have to improve substantially. I would expect whoever takes over to accept my calls—and to be available to see me."

The other man got the point at once. "Of course, Mr. Noble," he said faintly. "I will tell reception to put all calls through at once. There will be no more…delays."

"Good." Brand rose to his feet. Clea stood, too, and placed her fingertips on his arm. Pleasure surged through Brand, along with a very male desire at the contact against his bare skin. He felt ten feet tall and invincible. Reclaiming his assets and regaining his financial standing were secondary to the touch of her fingers. This was the first move she'd made in public to align herself with him, and the small gesture was a significant victory. He placed his hand over hers, holding it in place.

Once outside the bank, he couldn't contain his triumph. He grinned down at her. "What a self-satisfied ass."

She squeezed the arm she still held. "That's why I changed banks. He always made me feel…inadequate."

Brand slowed and turned to face her. She came to an abrupt halt, tilting her head back, her rosy lips slightly parted.

Lust surged through Brand. She'd never looked more desirable.

"Never feel inadequate. He's not worthy of your time. Forget about him, Dr. Noble—the man clearly has no brains." Gently he brushed a wayward curl out of her eyes. "Have dinner with me tonight," he said abruptly. "Let's go somewhere—"

"I can't," she interrupted, her eyes darkening. "I'm sorry, Brand, but I'm having dinner with…with a friend. It was arranged last week—before you came back. I can't cancel this late."

"No," he said tonelessly, determined not to show his disappointment. As her hand fell away from his arm, he shoved his hands into the pockets of his jeans. "Of course you can't."

Without waiting for her next response, he said, "I have a lot of catching up to do—starting with buying a decent cell phone. Then there's office space to secure, staff to hire." He glanced down at the black T-shirt and jeans and grimaced. "And clothes to buy."

"Shopping never was your favorite occupation." Clea's

mouth softened, then she glanced at the dainty platinum watch on her wrist. "I have meetings scheduled all afternoon. If you want, I could come with you later, after I'm done for the day...before I go out."

The pleasure that had filled him earlier had dissipated. Brand shook his head. "I'll be fine. You clear your calendar. Use the extra time to get ready for your dinner."

As Brand walked away, he left her staring after him, and he sensed that an opportunity to reconnect with his wife had been lost.

Next time, he vowed, he would not let such an opportunity slip past.

Eight

"You're going to kill me when you hear what I've done," Clea told Harry that evening as soon as the maitre d' had settled them at a table beside open sash windows that allowed the summer evening air to drift over them.

"Kill you?" Harry grinned at her over the menu he'd opened. "Never."

"Just wait," she said darkly. "I promise I'll change your mind."

"Why? What did you do this time?"

"This time?" objected Clea. Her order decided, she set the menu down. "That makes it sound like I regularly get into scrapes, and I'd like to remind you that when we were younger it was *you* who were always in trouble!"

"I've reformed," Harry said piously.

Clea snorted in disbelief. "Just gotten better at concealing it."

"Unfair! Remember who had to break the news of your marriage to your father?"

"I remember," she said with feeling.

How could she ever forget? Her father had been furious, even though Harry tried his best to run interference on behalf of her and Brand. His help had only exacerbated her father's rage. Clea ended up wishing she hadn't given in to Harry's suggestion to do her dirty work, and broken the news herself. She'd been so feeble in those days. But then she'd been young...and naive.

"So what *have* you done now?"

She groaned and dropped her chin into cupped hands. "Brand thinks the baby is yours."

Harry did a double take. "He thinks *what?*"

Clea bit her lip. "He thinks I'm pregnant with your child."

"That's what you told him?"

It was difficult to gauge Harry's reaction. For the first time in her life, Clea couldn't read him. He certainly wasn't as irritated as she'd expected. But neither was he laughing. "Not quite."

"So how did he get it so wrong?"

She started to feel awkward. "It's hard to explain."

"Try."

"Brand was being...difficult." How best to make Harry understand why she'd done it? "He assumed—"

"That I was your boyfriend?" Harry closed his menu and put it down. "And you didn't correct him?"

Clea wriggled uncomfortably in her seat. "I...he was behaving like a jerk."

"Clea! This is almost as crazy as your mad idea to have a baby in the first place."

"Harry, please." Clea reached for a linen napkin,

unfolded it and laid it on her lap. "I've had enough recriminations about that from Dad. Can we not go there?"

Leaning back in his chair, Harry assessed her. "So how did Brand react?"

"How do you imagine he reacted?"

"Badly," said Harry, waving away the waiter approaching to take their order.

She nodded. "That's an understatement."

"Poor Clea."

That made her feel even more wretched. "Of course, I'm going to have to tell him that it's not true. It's not fair to embroil you in…" Clea couldn't think of the right word to describe the bitter divide that separated her and Brand so she finally settled for "…our problems." What should've been a time of happiness with Brand back, had become riddled with bitterness and turmoil.

"Clea…" Harry pulled his chair around the table and draped an arm across her shoulders. "I hate to see you like this. We've been friends for a long time, right?"

She nodded, afraid to speak in case the tears that thickened the back of her throat spilled out.

"Remember that time I drank too much at William Hartwell's wedding reception and got pounced on by his beaky-nosed cousin? The one everyone except drunk ol' me knew was looking for a meal ticket to keep her in Moët and truffles for the rest of her life?"

She choked back a sound that was half laugh, half sob. "That was different. You were incapacitated—I had to rescue you from a fate worse than death."

"You told me I owed you."

"You do!"

The memory caused Clea to smile wanly. If looks could have fried, William's cousin would've have incinerated her on the spot.

Harry leaned forward. "So see this as repayment. Take advantage of me—let Brand continue to think you're carrying my baby. You don't have to tell him the truth right away. Give yourself some space, and choose the right time to tell him."

Harry had a point.

Clea had always reacted on impulse…and it hadn't always served her well. Even deciding to have the baby had been a heartfelt reaction to the chasm Brand's absence had left in her life, an attempt to build the family they'd discussed. She'd so badly needed something…*someone*… to give meaning to her life.

Conceiving the baby had done that.

If she did as Harry suggested and continued to let Brand believe that Harry was her baby's father a little longer, then Brand would also keep believing that Harry was her lover. It would be easier to keep him at a distance, making it far less likely that Brand would pick up on her body's humiliating reaction to him. It would give her a mask to hide behind.

Which reminded her…

"Um…there's something else you should know."

"What?"

"I told Brand we planned to get married."

Harry stared at her in disbelief, and then gave a shout of laughter that caused heads at the neighboring tables to turn. "Too funny."

"See? I've already taken advantage of you."

Clea didn't want to face up to the fact that she also wanted to make Brand sweat just a little. After all, he'd vanished for four years without explanation with a woman he'd never bothered to tell her he'd once lived with. Yet last night he'd so clearly expected her to crawl into bed with him in spite of all the distrust and tension simmering between them. Brand deserved to suffer—for a while.

But she had no intention of allowing him to permanently believe Harry was her baby's father.

"Use me as your human shield for as long as you want. Let Brand believe you intend to file for a divorce." Harry beckoned to the waiter hovering a distance away.

On cue Clea picked up her menu, though food was the last thing on her mind right now. "A human shield is exactly what I need," she told him with deep relief.

Harry as protection would help her to resist her attraction to Brand, though she wouldn't go as far as telling Brand she wanted a divorce yet. It might be weak-minded of her, but it would certainly be effective. Already she could feel an easing of the strain that had settled over her since Brand's return. "Harry, you're the best friend a woman could want."

He gave her a bittersweet smile. "Anytime. Now I deserve some champagne to celebrate our so-called engagement."

When Brand heard a car purr to a stop outside he found himself on his feet, stomach muscles tightening with expectation, as he cocked his head, listening for the lilt of Clea's voice.

Brand had finally conceded that Clea was right: Perhaps they had not communicated enough in the past. He'd considered the communication they shared in the bedroom enough. He'd told her how he felt with actions, not words. But now he was starting to realize that there were things they should've discussed. However difficult that might be for him.

Tonight he planned to begin building a bridge across the chasm of unspoken hurt and broken promises that lay

The Reader Service—Here's how it works:

Accepting your 2 free books and 2 free gifts (gifts valued at approximately $10.00) places you under no obligation to buy anything. You may keep the books and gifts and return the shipping statement marked "cancel." If you do not cancel, about a month later we'll send you 6 additional books and bill you just $4.30 each in the U.S. or $4.99 each in Canada. That is a savings of at least 14% off the cover price. It's quite a bargain! Shipping and handling is just 50¢ per book in the U.S. and 75¢ per book in Canada.* You may cancel at any time, but if you choose to continue, every month we'll send you 6 more books, which you may either purchase at the discount price or return to us and cancel your subscription.

*Terms and prices subject to change without notice. Prices do not include applicable taxes. Sales tax applicable in N.Y. Canadian residents will be charged applicable taxes. Offer not valid in Quebec. All orders subject to credit approval. Credit or debit balances in a customer's account(s) may be offset by any other outstanding balance owed by or to the customer. Please allow 4 to 6 weeks for delivery. Offer available while quantities last.

If offer card is missing write to: The Reader Service, P.O. Box 1867, Buffalo, NY 14240-1867 or visit us at www.ReaderService.com.

NO POSTAGE
NECESSARY
IF MAILED
IN THE
UNITED STATES

BUSINESS REPLY MAIL
FIRST-CLASS MAIL   PERMIT NO. 717   BUFFALO, NY

POSTAGE WILL BE PAID BY ADDRESSEE

THE READER SERVICE
PO BOX 1867
BUFFALO NY 14240-9952

Play the Lucky Hearts Game

and get...
2 FREE BOOKS and
2 FREE MYSTERY GIFTS...
YOURS TO KEEP!

yes! I have scratched off the gold card.
Please send me my *2 FREE BOOKS* and
2 FREE MYSTERY GIFTS (gifts are worth about $10).
I understand that I am under no obligation to purchase
any books as explained on the back of this card.

Scratch Here!
Then look below to see what your
cards get you....2 Free Books
& 2 Free Mystery Gifts!

225/326 HDL FJDQ

FIRST NAME

LAST NAME

ADDRESS

APT.#

CITY

STATE/PROV.

ZIP/POSTAL CODE

Visit us online at
www.ReaderService.com

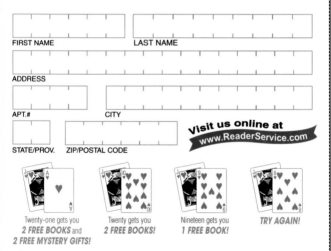

Twenty-one gets you
2 FREE BOOKS and
2 FREE MYSTERY GIFTS!

Twenty gets you
2 FREE BOOKS!

Nineteen gets you
1 FREE BOOK!

TRY AGAIN!

© 2011 HARLEQUIN ENTERPRISES LIMITED. Printed in the U.S.A.

▼ DETACH AND MAIL CARD TODAY! ▼

H-D-11/11

between them. To that end, he'd given Curtis the night off, to make sure he would be alone with Clea. The butler had initially protested, but Brand told him that after four years' absence, he needed time alone with his wife. To Brand's relief, Smythe had walked Curtis out. Now two mugs of chocolate—hot and frothy, just as Clea had always liked it—stood steaming on the butler's tray.

The sound of male laughter was unwelcome.

Brand strode out of the study into the hallway just as the front door access code bleeped.

Clea came through the door laughing, her hair thick and glossy, her mouth curved up in a smile. Emotion stabbed Brand. He'd missed her sparkle. Her joy. Behind her followed…Hall-Lewis.

Brand glared daggers at Clea, every male instinct on red-hot alert. So much for dinner with a friend. This wasn't the girlfriend he'd anticipated. His own fault! He'd allowed himself to be lulled into a false sense of security.

"Oh." Her mouth formed a perfect circle. "You're still up."

"I was waiting for you," he growled.

"Clea, is there a problem?" Hall-Lewis came up behind Clea and placed his hands on her shoulders.

"No problem," Brand said through gritted teeth. "Not now that you're leaving."

He heard Clea's gasp and there was an instant's utter silence.

Then Clea rushed to speak. "Brand, there's no need to be rude to—"

"Clea, that was a wonderful evening." Hall-Lewis smoothly overrode her protests. "I'll call you tomorrow and we can arrange a time for you to choose a ring."

"Harry, don't worry—"

"Or if you're too busy, I can choose a diamond to match the stars in your eyes."

Hall-Lewis chuckled. Brand fisted his hands at his sides. The man couldn't have made it clearer that he was much more considerate of Clea's workload than Brand had been yesterday.

When the other man's hands stroked along the curve of Clea's shoulders, down her slender arms, before turning her deftly and bending forward to kiss her, Brand shut his eyes so tightly stars danced on the backs of his eyelids. *He and Clea needed to talk.*

Brand opened his eyes to find Hall-Lewis watching him over Clea's glossy head, his face alight with triumph. Brand's hands hurt with the force of clenching them as he fought to keep his fists at his sides. But there was no reason not to glare straight back.

War had been declared.

The silence that followed in the wake of Harry Hall-Lewis's departure wrapped Brand in a viselike hold. "I need a drink," he muttered.

With a hollow sensation filling his chest, Brand headed down the high-ceilinged corridor and pushed open the door to the study that had once been his domain. The desk light was on, as well as a tall lamp beside the comfortable brown chesterfield couch where he'd sat earlier, reading, while he waited for Clea to return. The room bore evidence of Clea's occupation in his absence—a slim gold pen on the desk, a needlepoint cushion on his chesterfield, a shelf of novels that hadn't been there when he'd left—but essentially the room had remained the same, right down to the liquor cabinet in the far corner.

Clea was right on his heels as he opened the leaded-glass door of the cabinet. She ignored the mugs of hot chocolate he'd painstakingly prepared—they were still steaming on the butler's tray beside the sofa.

"Do you really think that's wise?" Clea asked. "Don't you think we should discuss what just happened back in the hallway without alcohol clouding the issue?"

There was no way in hell he was discussing the primal instincts that had risen within him when he'd seen her with her lover. And he certainly wasn't admitting the deathly animosity that had passed between him and Hall-Lewis.

Or the bone-deep certainty that had settled in his gut.

Clea was his. And he was not about to let her go, even though she carried Hall-Lewis's baby. Brand intended to reclaim his wife. *His* wife. She was not Hall-Lewis's fiancée—and would never be his bride.

He and Clea still had a marriage—and that negated whatever unholy deal she'd struck with Hall-Lewis. Besides she wasn't even wearing the man's ring yet. Of course, she wasn't wearing Brand's ring, either, but he'd remedy that later. Right now there was only one thing on Brand's mind: convincing Clea that she belonged with him.

Fortunately, Clea was oblivious to all the undercurrents that had swirled between him and Harry, or the turmoil tumbling around inside his head. But Brand had decided that Clea was right about one thing...they needed to talk. And now wasn't the ideal time—he needed time to cool down.

He slid Clea a covert look. "Is that offer to help me choose clothes still open?"

Surprise flitted across her face. "Of course."

Turning toward her, Brand exhaled in relief. "Good. We can go shopping in the morning and have lunch afterward." Clea didn't know it yet, but there would be only one outcome to the coming discussion: Hall-Lewis was history.

With Clea in front of him, Brand gazed down into the face he'd missed so much, and desire for her overwhelmed him.

"I made you a cup of hot chocolate." It came out husky. He inhaled the scent of her, as fresh and fragrant as he remembered. Unspoiled. "It's next to the couch."

"Thank you." Clea veered away, breaking the spell.

His hands shaking, Brand reached into the cabinet and poured himself two fingers of Irish whiskey—perhaps it would numb the impact of Clea's heady jasmine perfume. Making his way past her without yanking her into his arms and annihilating the kiss Hall-Lewis had placed on her lips took a huge amount of self-control. But he accomplished it. Once safely seated back on the chesterfield, Brand leaned his head back and sighed, a short, sharp burst of sound.

"Tired?"

Brand looked up. Clea was standing in front of him. A smudge of cream from the hot chocolate coated her top lip. *How sweet it would be to lick that away.* "You should go to bed," he told her brusquely. Before he acted on the explosive cocktail of rising desire and the sheer, possessive rage he'd felt at the sight of Hall-Lewis's hands all over her.

Mine.

He stopped himself from shouting it.

"I'll go as soon as I finish my chocolate." Clea stretched and yawned. Then fluttering her hand in front of her mouth, she murmured, "Sorry."

God, the last thing on *his* mind was sleep.

The cushion gave beside him as Clea dropped down onto the couch.

Brand didn't dare look at her. His senses went on high

alert. He was acutely aware of the overloud ticking of the antique grandfather clock in the corner of the room and the sweet feminine scent that surrounded Clea. His whole existence funneled into the present. And the two of them.

He took a gulp of the whiskey he no longer wanted.

"I'd already agreed to go to dinner with Harry before you came back," she said from beside him.

"I know. You told me that." What was wrong with the woman? He didn't want to talk about her night out with *Harry*. To lighten the mood before she figured him for a basket case, he said, "I had a great-aunt who had a Bassett hound called Harry. It had great big red eyes that looked like it had spent all night in tears."

"Brand!" But she sounded like she was smiling. "Harry doesn't have red, teary eyes."

Yet.

But that could change if Brand had anything to do with it.

Brooding, Brand set his nearly full glass down on the low, square table beside the couch and turned his head.

She *was* smiling. The edges of her mouth had curled up, and her eyes sparkled. The power of that smile lit up her whole face.

Heat shot through Brand. He wanted to hear her laugh again—the same joyous sound that had shot a lightning bolt of hot emotion through him when she'd come in through the front door with Harry behind her.

He could still make her laugh, couldn't he? He could certainly try. "Who calls a grown man Harry, for God's sake? It's a name for dogs and hamsters."

The corners of her mouth stayed up-tilted. "Don't forget wizarding heroes and princes. It's very distinguished—it's short for Henry."

"That begs the question. Who calls a son Henry?"

"It's got to be better than calling a daughter Cleopatra." Before he could tell her he liked her name, she continued, "Lots of queens called their babies *Henry*. Many kings of England are Henry."

Brand gave a snort and laid an arm along the back of the sofa behind her head, taking care not to touch her. Not yet. "I doubt it was the queen's call. You're telling me Hall-Lewis has royal aspirations?"

She gave a gurgle of laughter. A real laugh that kept his gaze on her mouth.

"Of course not! And stop calling him Hall-Lewis—it's such a mouthful."

"There won't be any need to call him anything at all if he continues to paw you," he said darkly.

"He wasn't pawing me!"

"His hands were all over you." Brand came up on the couch and moved closer.

Clea averted her face until he could only see a slice of flushed cheek beyond the veil of her curls.

"You're overreacting, Brand."

"Overreacting?" The light and laughter had vanished. All Brand could focus on was the telling fact that Clea hadn't told her lover to stop, only him—her husband.

The dangerous possessive heat, so close to the surface, spun out of control. Acting on the outrage and anger bottled up within him, Brand clasped her shoulders and swung her around to face him. "Did you enjoy it when *he* stroked your shoulders like this?" he snarled, matching actions to his words. Yet the instant his fingers brushed against her skin, a different, more intense, yet more poignant emotion, wiped out all anger.

Ah, hell!

She stiffened then stilled when his fingers gently settled

into the lightest, stroking touch. Her eyes widened, the pupils darkening as she stared at him.

"Or when he kissed you…"

Brand didn't wait to add *like this*. He simply acted.

The taste of her was intoxicating. Sweet chocolate. And, more tantalizing, the taste that was the essence of Clea. Honey. Jasmine. Brand hit an instant high, adrenaline pumping through his bloodstream. He sampled the sweetness, licked the chocolate froth from her top lip, felt her shift restlessly against him.

He hauled her off the leather couch, into his lap and sealed his mouth across hers, claiming her as *his*.

Brand was conscious of the roughness of his desert-callused fingertips against her silken skin. It highlighted the difference between them…and heightened his arousal. She was so beautiful. So sweet. So soft. *His* Clea.

Once he'd started, he couldn't stop. Nor did she object as he smoothed his hand along her leg under the fabric of the dress she wore. The skin covering her inner thigh was sleek and smooth. He caressed the silkiness in circular motions, until she bit back a half moan. His fingers inched under the edge of her panties. Clea's breath caught—a harsh, jagged sound in the silence broken only by the tick of the grandfather clock.

His fingers retreated and returned to the silky skin. "You're so incredibly soft."

He pressed openmouthed kisses along the seam of her lips until they parted, yet still he didn't sink into the welcoming sweetness to explore more deeply. Inside he was shaking. A mass of desperate, hungry urges. Yet he held off, deferring the pleasure, waiting for her to initiate the action.

She moved in his lap, the curve of her bottom rubbing against the erection restrained by his denim jeans. Brand groaned at the agony of having her so close. He wanted to thrust his tongue into her mouth, yank her skirt up and rip the scraps of lace she called underwear off. He wanted to part her legs and ream his ready hardness into the feminine heat that he'd been deprived of for so long.

It would be over in seconds.

A terrible letdown for Clea…

Hardly the way to start their life over again. He fought for restraint, and touched her inner thigh with trembling fingers. His hand slid higher and found moist, slick flesh. *She was ready.* Blood rushed through him, making him light-headed. He stroked with slow care that belied the primal instincts pounding through him, and she arched up against him, her breathing quickening.

Her heart thudded against his chest. Brand wished they were naked. He wanted her skin bare against his so he could absorb her heartbeat. The barriers of his T-shirt and her silk dress were sheer torture.

"Open your legs."

For a heartbeat she didn't respond—and Brand thought he'd pushed too fast. Tense, he waited for her to leap off his lap and flee.

Then she moved, and his heart seized. Her legs splayed across his lap, offering him access to delights he'd dreamed of in the darkness of his desert cell, only to waken and find them nothing but a cruel mirage. Leaving him feeling sullied, beset by the fear that his love for Clea had been defiled by bringing her memory into his violent world.

But this…touching her…was like the first time, that first night, all those years ago.

Except now she was his wife—and this time he knew exactly how to pleasure her. Even though there was more uncertainty and fear than there'd ever been in those heady, halcyon days when he'd first courted Clea.

It was different now. No fairy-tale romance. No head-long falling in love.

This was raw…

And very, very real.

Her mouth slanted over his and her tongue swept in. *At last.* She'd done it—she'd made the move he'd been waiting for. Brand suppressed a male roar of approval. Instead he rewarded her with little sucking nips. She squirmed against him.

Brand stroked more deeply, his fingers testing the slick channel between her parted legs, even as her breath caught.

"Let go, let it happen," he murmured.

"Aah."

The gasp that broke from her roused an emotion in Brand that he thought he'd lost forever. He swallowed against the thick, painful lump in his throat and stroked again, his fingers gentle. Her body leaped, superbly responsive to his touch.

The control he'd fought so hard to leash was finally stripped. *She was his.* Brand drove two fingers into her. Clea gasped, her head fell back and the shudders started.

Nine

Clea could barely bring herself to look at Brand during the ride to Madison Avenue on Saturday morning. Much good her human shield had done…at Brand's first touch, she'd surrendered.

Totally.

Even looking out the window, she was tautly, intensely aware of the man beside her. Brand had been perusing the papers when she'd come downstairs this morning, desperately hoping he might already have left. No such luck.

When she'd entered the breakfast room, he'd tossed his reading aside, speared her with a look and offered a terse greeting—which had done nothing to soothe her already ragged nerves.

Brand looked as cool as ice.

She started to ache. What had happened between them last night hadn't been about love…it had been about sex.

During the drive he'd said little, which had only added to the antsy feeling stringing her out. So when Smythe held the back door of the Lincoln open for her to alight, Clea bulleted out onto the sidewalk and into the small, exclusive menswear outfitters.

What must Brand think of her?

Clea stopped in front of a rack of suits and shuddered at the blazing flashes of memory from last night that she'd just as soon forget.

Staring blindly at the selection of finely tailored garments, she could only agonize over how her very worst fear had materialized. Even with all the unresolved issues between herself and Brand, the uncertainty, the lack of trust…it had taken only one touch, and she'd fallen into his arms. Worse than that, she couldn't blame Brand for what had happened—she hadn't even tried to resist after he'd kissed her.

As soon as she'd come to her senses, she'd made a hasty, lame excuse of being tired, even though she'd been aware that he must be on fire. But her guilt had been outgunned by her need to escape. Thankfully, Brand had taken her excuse at face value…and Clea made a run for the guest bedroom.

She still wasn't sure whether she'd bolted the door to lock Brand out—or to keep herself in. But his footfalls hadn't even paused outside on his way to bed, while she'd lain awake for hours reliving the entire episode over and over in her mind.

How she'd all but attacked him, climbing astride him, kissing him…demanding—

"Can I help you?"

The question caused her to swing around. Heat suffusing her cheeks, Clea blinked at the dapper man standing in front of her, a discreet name tag proclaimed him to be Alberto.

"Uh…"

Brand moved soundlessly to flank Alberto. "Is Emilio in today?"

"Emilio retired and sold the business to me two years ago. I'm his cousin—the store has stayed in the family."

Brand's face wore a strange expression. "Once again life has moved on. I need clothes. Let's start with two suits," he continued, without missing a beat. "I'll need shirts and sportswear, too."

The salesman's eyes lit up at the prospect. "I'll take you to the fitting rooms, then I'll bring the garments."

While Alberto quickly measured Brand's leg length and waist size, Clea studied the fitting room. A large mirror took up one wall. The carpet, in an oatmeal shade that matched the tint of the walls, should've given the area a spacious feel. Yet as soon as Alberto shut the fitting-room door behind him, Clea became aware of the suffocating proximity.

Brand reached to grab the back of his white T-shirt and pulled it over his head in one smooth movement, leaving his upper body naked. Clea stared. His biceps bulged and his chest was broad—the pectoral muscles more defined than she remembered—sloping down to a trim, lean waist. His skin gleamed like polished oak.

Then his hand reached for the zipper of his jeans.

Clea swallowed. She hadn't considered that he'd be taking off his clothes when she'd offered to accompany him shopping.

She chickened out. "I'll go see if Alberto needs any help with color selections," she said, wrenching the door open.

Coward.

But it was worth the relief she felt, Clea decided, as her hot discomfort subsided. If she carried on like this, Brand was going to know how much he affected her—and she couldn't afford that. Not when he no longer loved her.

But he still wants you, taunted a wicked little voice. *Remember last night?*

No. She would not think about last night.

Clea marched across the shop to where she could see Alberto adding a garment to the stack draped over his left arm. Her phone beeped, and she extracted it from her purse. She'd missed three calls. Her father. Harry. And a book-club friend. No doubt her father wanted to invite Harry and her over. The three of them often spent Saturday afternoons or evenings together. Clea glanced toward the fitting room.

Brand had invited her to lunch.

They needed to talk. She hesitated then came to a decision. She switched her phone off then slid it back into her purse. She'd call back. Later.

Looking up, she saw Alberto had already selected three suits and an armful of business shirts. "Italian styling—rather than French—for your man," he told Clea. "More powerful. Less refined."

Clea smiled in acknowledgment, and Alberto headed for the fitting room.

It was easy to see why Brand came to this establishment. Alberto was efficient and competent, as Emilio must have been. No doubt Brand had known he would be in and out of here in the shortest time possible.

So why had Brand suggested that she come with him? Clearly he didn't need her help. Scanning the shelves of immaculately arranged shirts, Clea's gaze landed on a display of ties and belts. To give herself time, she headed over to inspect them. Had the invitation been an elaborate cover-up to persuade her to have lunch with him, when she'd turned down his dinner invite? Had this been the easiest way to get what he wanted?

If he'd only asked her to dinner, he would've gotten what he wanted. She wouldn't have refused.

But the way Brand's mind worked had always been a mystery to her. So controlled…so contained…so secretive.

Drawing a deep breath as she mulled over his motives, Clea selected two belts she thought Brand might like, then returned to the fitting room. Hovering in the doorway, she saw that Brand had already donned a pair of suit pants and a white shirt, which he was busy tucking in while Alberto pinned the trouser cuffs. Clea gave a silent sigh of relief. Clothed, he posed far less of a threat to her peace of mind—yet he was still every inch the powerful, irresistible male. And, with Alberto there, too, the oppressive intimacy in the fitting room had dissipated.

The tightness in her chest began to ease.

"The fit of these trousers is good." Brand placed his hands on his hips and turned to face her. There was nothing in his expression to show that he had any idea why she'd rushed out.

Clea followed his lead. "I thought you might need a belt."

"Thanks." Brand reached out and took the slightly narrower of the two. His fingers brushed her hand, and Clea struggled to keep her breathing even. *This was how the trouble had started last night…with a touch.*

The bell sounded from the front of the shop, and Alberto excused himself. Instantly, the thick tension was back in full force. Brand continued to thread the belt through the loops in his trousers, apparently unaffected. Yet Clea couldn't help noticing how the fit of his pants showed off his lean waist…

Help! "Perhaps a slightly narrower belt?" Her voice sounded strangled. "I'll go look for one."

"That's not necessary. This one's fine." Brand pulled the leather through the buckle with a snap. Reaching for the suit jacket, he shrugged it on carelessly then flexed his shoulders, causing the fabric to grow taunt.

Clea's breath snagged in her throat as he turned to face her. The dark gray of the suit provided a foil for his startling aqua eyes. For an instant she felt as though he could see right into her soul...read her every secret.

It disturbed her.

Forcing herself to ignore the wretched image, she said brightly, "You look like a million dollars. It's perfect." Her eye landed on the collar. "Oh, just one sec."

He gave her a crooked smile. "Maybe not a million dollars?"

Act unconcerned. Crossing over to stand behind him, she reached for his shirt collar. Brand had gone as still as a statue. Clea's heart started to pound again. Perhaps this hadn't been her best idea; she should've stayed in the relatively safe zone of the doorway. Her fingers had turned to thumbs, and she fiddled to straighten the recalcitrant collar.

"There." Her voice was husky. "Definitely a million dollars. Look at yourself." Turning her head when she got no response, she discovered Brand watching her in the mirror. A frisson of shock stabbed her as their eyes tangled.

"A million dollars," he repeated, holding her gaze.

Desire, hot and molten, chased panic through her veins. *Run.* But it was too late to obey the fight-or-flight impulse. Brand spun around, a blur of movement too fast for her eye to follow. This time their eyes clashed without the false reflection of the mirror…and this time Brand was right in front of her. Clea's lips parted.

Brand made a sound that was half groan, half laugh. "You do realize that if I kiss you now, I'll never stop."

"You'll have to stop. You still have to try on the other two suits." Beneath the prosaic statement, Clea's voice was hoarse with hunger.

"One kiss."

It had taken only one touch to land her in hell last night.

A door banged shut. Someone—Alberto?—called out a greeting. Clea jumped back, quickly retreating to the doorway. "Brand. Not here—not now."

Not anywhere. Not anytime. But Clea knew it was already far too late for that. She was trembling as she grasped the frame of the doorway and Brand's breathing sounded loud in the private space. They were both far past the point of no return. And she knew what was happening between them was as inevitable as the sunrise in the morning.

Nothing could protect her.

Except him.

After a long shuddering moment, Brand said, "Okay, not now…but later."

With a safe distance of five feet between them, Clea watched him warily through her lashes. "But first we talk."

"You drive a hard bargain, woman." Brand gave her an indecipherable look. "I'll hold you to it."

As shivers shook her, Clea silently hoped she hadn't let herself in for more than she could handle.

It had taken Brand a little over an hour to replenish his wardrobe, much to Clea's obvious consternation.

After picking out three suits and a week's worth of business shirts, Brand arranged for the suits to be delivered to the house once the tailoring had been completed. Then he'd allowed Clea to drag him to the new Cesare Attolini store, before finishing off at Ralph Lauren, where, in less than fifteen minutes, he'd rounded up three pairs of denims and a half-dozen T-shirts and Polo shirts along with a pair of sneakers. He donned a pair of jeans and a shirt then paid for the rest, without bothering to try them on. Before Clea could object, he'd told her that what didn't fit could easily be exchanged, leaving Clea shaking her head and muttering about men being from Mars.

But Brand had had enough of shopping, of crowds, of being unable to catch more than a quick glimpse of blue sky as they exited one store and entered the next. The buildings were closing in on him. He needed space. A walk through the green oasis of Central Park to the Loeb Boathouse Restaurant provided the perfect antidote to the restlessness consuming him.

They were escorted to a table at the lake's edge. Once they were seated, the tranquil water beside them, Brand scrutinized Clea from behind the menu. He took in the small frown of concentration crinkling her brow—and the way the leaf-green top she wore accentuated her eyes.

Brand had deliberately chosen the Boathouse Restaurant for lunch. One of their old haunts, he intended to reawaken memories of the good times they'd shared, though it would be important to keep a cool head during the discussion to come. He was fighting for everything that mattered most.

After all, Clea was still his wife.

And he wasn't about to allow that to change. Whatever Hall-Lewis planned.

When the waiter returned for their order, Brand shut his menu with a snap—he hadn't needed to peruse the menu to know precisely what he wanted: the familiar comfort of a burger with a cold Coca-Cola. It had been too long since he'd enjoyed such mundane Western pleasures. And it took Clea only a few seconds extra to decide on wild mushroom ravioli and a green salad.

"When I was young I used to imagine celebrating my wedding day here beside the lake," Clea said dreamily after the waiter departed.

The information came out of the blue, and Brand's interest sharpened. "I always knew you enjoyed coming here—but you never told me that before."

"It's so romantic—see how the water reflects the trees. The rowboats. The swans. The gondolier." A skimming gesture of Clea's arm encompassed the scene. "Even the city skyline in the distance beyond the trees reminds you that it's a secret world in the middle of New York City."

Brand followed the arc of her arm, his gaze skimming over the glass-smooth surface of the water to where the lone gondolier punted near a bridge.

The waiter came back and poured sparkling mineral water into a tulip glass for Clea before setting a tall, frosted glass of cola in front of Brand. After the waiter had hurried off, Clea's voice grew softer. "And I never said anything to you because I never wanted you worrying that I'd missed out by getting married in Vegas."

But she *had* missed out. Clea had deserved the romantic white wedding of her girlhood fantasies. Hell, she'd even been a virgin. Brand's body tightened as he remembered the disbelief—and devotion—that had overwhelmed him when he'd made that surprise discovery on their wedding night—as unexpected as discovering a mythical unicorn in a modern world.

Her hand lightly touched his arm. Brand stiffened as tingles of electric awareness skated over his skin, and he focused on her slender fingers with their short, perfectly manicured nails.

"Anyway, you asked me to marry you in Central Park, remember?" she said. "Before we rushed off to Vegas. So you must have sensed my tie to this place."

Of course he'd felt it. Against his tanned forearm, the bare mark on her third finger where her ring—his ring—should've rested mocked him. Brand raised his gaze to meet hers. "The heat was stifling. I proposed to you under an oak—it was the deepest shade we could find."

"I remember." Her eyes grew unexpectedly misty and her hand tightened on his arm.

Brand sucked in a deep breath as heat shafted through him. After a pause that was filled by the chatter from the surrounding tables, he pointedly stroked his thumb over the lighter groove of skin. "Clea, I'd like you to wear your wedding ring again—after all, we are still married."

The soft dreaminess vanished as Clea slowly shook her head. "I can't."

Her refusal hit Brand like a blow in the gut.

Before he could respond, their meals arrived. Brand removed his hand and waited for Clea to tuck into her ravioli, then followed suit with his own burger. They ate in silence, the clink of cutlery and the hum of conversation from the surrounding tables filling the space between them.

As Brand pondered her refusal to wear her ring again, he realized that it shouldn't have come as a surprise. After he'd carefully chewed and swallowed the last mouthful of burger, he said, "We need to talk about Harry."

"Harry?" Clea's eyebrows arched upward. She set her knife and fork down together on her empty plate. "What do you want to discuss?"

Brand narrowed his gaze. "You can hardly marry the man while you're still married to me." Clea started to say something, and he cut her off. "I'm not dead, so our marriage stands. You need to know I'm not going to agree to a neat, tidy divorce."

"Brand—"

"So you need to reconsider this rash plan."

"It wasn't rash at all. You were gone. And I've known Harry for most of my life." She tipped her chin up in a gesture that was pure Clea and studied him with a frown, causing his chest to tighten with dread. "Much longer than I've known you, in fact."

"Time means nothing. You can know someone for years and know nothing about him...marriage changes everything."

A cloud passed over her face. "I married you within a month of meeting you, Brand. And even though we were married, and we spent most nights naked in each other's arms, I barely knew you." Clea paused for a breath, then continued. "Even though you told me you loved me, there was a part of you that you always kept hidden. You kept secrets."

It wasn't the first time she'd raised this issue, and it was starting to dawn on Brand that she might be right. But still he defended himself. "Some of those were very real secrets—military secrets I was not at liberty to reveal."

"Not all of them."

"No," Brand admitted. "But there were things—terrible things—that I preferred not to discuss, not to dwell on."

"Okay, I can accept that. But sometimes I sensed there was a distance between us that I would never cross. At first I put it down to the fact that you were older, and, as you say, that you had seen so much more than me. But that distance...your reserve formed an impenetrable wall...and made it difficult for me to truly understand you."

Brand didn't like the flat way she said that. "And you feel that you understand Harry?"

She gave a small smile that he liked even less. It held amusement…fondness.

"Harry adores me. And Harry would never lie to me—not even by omission."

"Are you sure about that?"

Clea blinked. "Absolutely!"

In an instant of turbulent clarity, Brand realized that their conversation had nothing to do with Harry. And everything to do with the unresolved, unspoken tension that writhed between them. The chasm of emotional distance that Clea was talking about. But still he dodged the issue. "That's why you want to marry Harry…because he says he loves you?"

Her response was immediate. "It's not the only reason. Harry's great father material."

Did that mean she thought he wasn't? Brand knew they'd reached break point. What happened the next few minutes would determine their future. Holding her gaze, he said softly, "But your baby already has a father figure—me! I will be the best father for your child that I can be." He gave her a narrow-eyed look. "Better than Hall-Lewis."

Clea rolled her eyes. "It's not a competition, Brand."

"Tell that to your friend, Harry," he growled.

"Harry's not like that. He's laid-back and easygoing." Clea didn't even blink as her eyes remained fixed on his.

An alien panic filled him. *He'd barely found her, and now he was going to lose her.* She wanted to talk. Yet he was struggling to open up in the way he knew she wanted. Why did men and woman have to be so damn different? Maybe it was different with Hall-Lewis. *That* filled him with ire. She trusted Hall-Lewis; clearly, she no longer trusted her husband. To him, his fear of losing Clea far outweighed the betrayal that had so angered him the night they'd been reunited. He could understand why she'd been drawn to Harry—he was her friend—and she thought Brand was dead. But he was back. And he had no intention of letting her go. Not in this lifetime.

"Clea, don't feel you have to marry Harry to give your baby a father. I will accept the baby."

"It could be yours—if you wanted."

Brand recoiled. Letting go of her hand, he stared across into turbulent green eyes. "You're talking adoption?"

For once he couldn't read her. Hell, he'd consider it, he'd do anything to keep her.

"We can discuss that later," she said in an odd voice. "We have enough to talk about already."

Brand nodded. "There's certainly plenty to discuss. Most importantly, I want you to tell Hall-Lewis there is no future for him. You're not going to marry him."

Clea's tongue tip touched her bottom lip.

His body reacted instantly to the sight of that bit of pink. Oh, Lord. She didn't need him to lust all over her. *Been there, done that. It was time to cut to the chase.*

Brand set his mouth in a hard line. "You know that Harry's bankrupt?"

The shock on Clea's face told him she hadn't.

"When did you have time to find that out?"

"I have my sources," he said mysteriously. Settling back in his chair, Brand lifted his glass and took a sip. Over the smooth rim, his eyes never leaving hers, he hammered home whatever advantage surprise might already have gained him. "Do you know that he was given sixty days to come up with a million dollars to temporarily stave off his creditors?"

She looked uncomfortable. "What are you driving at, Brand?"

"You're easily worth a million dollars to him. Marrying

you would be a simple solution to all Harry's financial problems."

Her fingers toyed with the stem of her glass. "'A million dollars.' This is what you were getting at back at the shop?" It hadn't been, but Brand let it slide as Clea continued more heatedly, "And that's the only reason Harry would want to marry me, right?"

"Of course not!" Brand started to reach for her hand, but she lifted her glass and stared at the bubbles rising in streams to the surface. Leaving his hand on the table, he said, "You've got a lot to offer Harry—you're a treasure beyond price to any man."

But he could see that Clea wasn't listening. She set the glass down and folded her linen napkin up, placing it with careful deliberation on the table.

When she looked up, her face was expressionless.

"I'm not going to marry Harry—I never was."

Relief lifted a ton of weight from him.

Brand had been so certain that she would be demanding a divorce. Family was important to Clea; he'd known she wouldn't want to keep her baby from its father. He'd read her wrong. "So why tell me you were marrying him?"

"When I saw you again…" Clea's voice trailed away. "In my fantasies I'd lived out the moment for years. But the reality was nothing like what I'd expected. You were so different—so hard, so angry. I needed time to think."

He'd caused his own downfall—but he'd been justified. Before he could defend himself, she started speaking again, so quietly he had to lean forward to catch her words. "Because if I really loved Harry it wouldn't matter that he was broke—because we'd have each other. That would give us all the riches I'd need."

She didn't love Hall-Lewis, at least not in any way that mattered! "Your trust fund would've helped."

Clea's green eyes started to spark. "Why does that always come up? And I'm not the one who keeps raising it."

"No, in the past it was your father, your friend Harry and your other society friends."

Her eyes widened as she registered the bitterness he could not hide. "I didn't think you'd noticed that they accused you of marrying me for my trust fund—"

"I noticed."

"I never believed it." She was examining him in a way Brand didn't like, as if she could see into his soul. Her eyes had gone all soft. "It hurt you!"

"Not hurt." Brand shook his head. "Annoyed me, like the whine of mosquitoes in the heat of the desert night."

Secretive. That's what she'd called him. Remote. Distant. He had been—but then she'd been so young. He hadn't wanted to worry her with his damnable suspicions. He would have to work on being more open....

He would have to start working on being a father, too. He'd learn to be the family man Clea wanted.

Her touch startled him. Clea had leaned forward, resting all five fingers of her left hand on his arm; she did it with a natural ease that Brand envied. *Hell, that's what he'd wanted to do.* It had become so hard to talk, to touch...

"You came from a large family. You went into the Special Air Services—became an expert at what you did. Then you discovered a passion for ancient artifacts and sought to learn everything you could about that. That's so much more admirable than being a trust-fund tycoon. It was your passion that drew me to you—you were different. That's why I fell in love with you."

Her honesty humbled Brand. The time had come to stop hiding, whatever it cost him.

Looking down at her slender fingers resting on his arm,

he placed his hand over hers. Then he met her eyes and gave her the naked truth shorn of all embellishments. "All I ever wanted was you."

Ten

"I don't understand," Clea said.

Brand didn't respond.

So she drew a shaky breath and, reluctant to reveal her inner insecurities to him, looked away across the lake to where a pair of swans paddled, leaving a trail of rippling water in their wake. "I thought there was someone else."

"Who? Anita?"

Hearing him say the other woman's name caused a flurry of fear. *What had she started?*

Once upon a time Clea had believed with all her heart—without a whisper of doubt—that Brand loved her. *Only her.* She'd loved him with an all-consuming passion that she'd never contemplated might be one-sided—even though he'd always been the most enigmatic and compelling man she'd ever met, and she hadn't always understood him.

But the Brand who'd returned no longer appeared

capable of loving her. There wasn't even a halfhearted pretense that he loved her. If another woman had taken her place, that would go a long way toward explaining the emotional changes in him.

"Come, let's walk." Brand was on his feet, and in a matter of minutes he'd paid for the meal and led her from the restaurant to a pathway that wound along the banks of the lake.

Out on the water, Clea could still see the pair of swans she'd been watching earlier. One had slowed, and was peering into the water, its neck a graceful arch. Behind, its mate had stopped to look, too. Marital bliss. She'd read somewhere that swans mated for life. Which brought her back to the uneasy relationship that simmered between her and Brand...

"*Is* it Anita? Or is there someone else?" she demanded, and her heart started to knock against her ribs as she waited apprehensively for his response.

"Someone else!"

The mocking way he said it, the inflection in his voice, caused her to flick him a sideways glance. One side of his mouth had kicked up.

Clea's temper slipped. She came to a standstill. "Damn you, Brand. Are you trying to humiliate me?"

His mouth twisted into a grimace and there was a strange expression in his eyes. If she hadn't known better, she might even have thought it was uncertainty. But that would be wrong, because Brand was the most confident person she'd ever met. He knew who he was—what he wanted from life—even though he mystified her.

"There is no other woman," he said. "Doesn't my desperate reaction to your touch tell you that much?"

Clea snorted in disbelief. "You can hardly bring yourself to touch me!"

"Not true. If I started, I'd never stop."

Her heart climbed into her throat. What was he saying? Dare she take him seriously? Surely he was laughing at her. He must be. But she had to know for sure. "What about Anita?"

He shrugged. "What about her?"

Clea did her best to hide the frustration, the desolation—the budding hope—that warred inside her, to keep her voice level as she explained, "The detective I hired after you went missing initially suspected that you were having an affair—he told me all the signs of infidelity were there." The only reaction Brand showed was the slightest narrowing of his eyes. It made him appear even more remote. But she'd started this—no point stopping now. So she plowed on, "He found evidence that you and Anita spent quite a bit of time together. In Greece. And, after the last time I spoke to you, you went to Iraq together."

Brand watched her through narrowed eyes. "Anita was a colleague. She was helping me with…a project."

"You never mentioned anything like that to me." And she'd had plenty of time in the days after it had sunk in that Brand had vanished to comb through their last weeks together, to rehash every conversation, every telephone call.

"You'd always been sensitive about her—I was reluctant to bring up her name."

"With good cause, apparently. You said you'd merely dated—when actually you'd lived together!"

"I was dumb. I admit that." Brand raised his shoulders and spread his hands. "You were unreasonably paranoid about the woman so I lied to stop you from fussing about her. I still worked with her…and I needed you to settle down and accept that. Later, it was too late to tell you the truth without creating a much bigger issue. I was sunk."

Clea had to admit that Brand had a point. He'd been her first love…and some sixth sense had alerted her to how attuned to each other Brand and Anita were. Much more so than a couple with a history of only a few dates. As an archaeologist, an expert on Middle Eastern antiquities, Anita had shared Brand's passion—making her more dangerous in Clea's eyes. In the early days, Brand had invited Anita to a dinner party at their home. Clea had felt threatened, barely responding to the woman's friendly overtures. Brand had known. Afterward he'd made love to her, reassured her, told her that he loved her. Only her. That Anita would never be more than a valued work consultant. And Clea had believed him.

After he'd gone missing—even after Clea had discovered that they'd been photographed together—she'd clung to that reassurance. Her father and Harry had clearly thought she was delusional. But to suspect Brand of betraying their marriage vows at that point would have plunged her into a chasm of despair that she'd been too frightened to contemplate.

"What was the project she was helping you with?" she finally asked.

Brand loosened the second button of his polo shirt and ran his finger around the collar, and Clea found her gaze drawn to the hollow below his throat. She watched him swallow and felt again the powerful tug of attraction.

"It no longer matters."

Pulling herself together, Clea said, "I think it does."

From his startled glance, she knew her dormant anger was showing. But Clea didn't care. In the past she'd been too besotted to question Brand when he'd brushed her off. He'd been older; she hadn't seen the danger of his secrecy.

"The project was confidential—it was jettisoned." He thrust his hands into the pockets of his suit pants and started to walk, his long strides eating up ground. "I never got a chance to see it through."

This was typical of the Brand she'd lived with. He'd never been big on explanations. In those days, it hadn't bothered her. But now it did. She'd changed…grown up. She wanted an equal partner. Not a husband who treated her like a child to be indulged at best or lived his life separately.

This time she was not going to be left on the other side of the divide.

Clea trotted after him. "Okay, so you can't give me details. But you *can* tell me where you were."

He shook his head. "You don't want to know."

"I do." When he remained silent, the tears that had been threatening finally overflowed. *"Damn you.* Do you have any idea what I've been through?"

Clea slowed, blinking furiously, and turned away, leaving the path, heading for the lake. A breeze ruffled the water's surface, breaking the mirror calm, and wafted across to the shore, but Clea barely noticed.

She sensed, rather than heard, Brand's approach.

Years of pent-up grief and simmering resentment got the better of her. "Not one word from you. In nearly four years couldn't you at least have let me know you were okay? That you were alive?" A sob broke from her tight throat. "Do you know how lonely I've been without you? How much uncertainty I've endured? How scared I've been?"

"Clea, I'm sorry." He caught her by the shoulders and she tensed. "I understand," he said with unexpected gentleness, turning her around to face him. "You don't have to justify yourself to me. I might not like it, but I can accept that you thought I was dead and you were lonely for comfort."

He still believed she'd slept with Harry.

Clea wanted to shake the weight of his hands off her shoulders, slap sense into him. Was it so hard for him to think outside the box and consider that she might not have needed a lover to get pregnant?

Her shoulders tense under his touch, she said, "Do you have any idea what it was like to live day after day trying to figure out why you'd left? Trying to understand what it was about me that made you decide to walk out and stay away for four years?" The lump in her throat was too thick to swallow past.

A shaft of sunlight caught the flex of a muscle high on his cheek. But, for once, Brand didn't retreat into that closed-off place where she couldn't follow.

"It was never like that."

"And since you've been back I've been growing more convinced that the investigators' initial assessment was correct—you deserted me for Anita." All her aching hurt was out in the open for him to see. "It's what everyone else thought from the beginning."

His hands smoothed along the rise of her shoulders and he cupped her face. "I haven't been holed up in a love nest. I was taken prisoner—for the first year I barely saw light."

Horror darkened Clea's eyes. "Brand! *Why?*"

"At first, I thought it was an opportunistic snatching and that Akam—the ring leader—assumed I was a wealthy foreigner and hoped to make a quick buck. When he kept uprooting the camp and moving deeper into the desert, I decided he'd gotten cold feet and feared reprisal."

"Yet you escaped?"

Brand shook his head. "In the first few months I planned to but there was no opportunity—I was guarded too closely. After that period we moved around. Later, I had more freedom—but by that stage I knew I would need resources to get out of Iraq. Akam and I had started to forge a relationship. He was being threatened. Keeping me became a danger to him. He had two choices—to kill me or to let me go."

Clea shuddered in his hold. "He let you go?"

"He helped me in the end. He was a Kurd, and came from a long line of smugglers. He arranged a ride for me to a spot north of Al Sulaymaniyah, where I was left with directions to reach a village in the mountains and a letter of introduction to a ring of smugglers who operated there. The plan was to accompany them over an ancient smugglers' route through the mountains into Turkey where he had a distant cousin who would provide me with a passport. The journey took a lot longer than it should have. The smugglers' route comes close to Iran and the border is unmarked. Our group was arrested for straying into Iran—and the horses and supplies were confiscated."

"Oh, Brand."

"We were held for several months before being released." Brand couldn't tell her about his relief that the Iranian border guards had considered him nothing more than a nuisance smuggler. He'd dared not speak or react, and so the border guards had considered him deaf and dumb. "I had sewn some money that Akam gave me into the waistband of my jeans—thankfully the guards didn't discover it. It was money I—and Akam—could ill afford to lose." Brand smiled. "I'd already promised to pay him back—with generous interest and a substantial bonus—he'd taken enough of a risk."

Her eyes were wide with shock. "That's terrible! I don't know how you can be so calm about it all."

"I had no choice—and I'm back now."

"I want to know it all—every detail."

Brand winced inwardly. He'd known this moment

would come. Next she'd be insisting on full details about why he'd been in Iraq in the first place. "Clea, here's my promise to you—I will tell you everything I know. But there are some things I need to straighten out for myself first. I need you to give me time."

"Of course I'll give you time. My God. I can't even begin to contemplate how traumatic the entire experience must have been." Clea dipped her chin against his fingers. "Take as much time as you need—I can wait. I'll be here."

Clea couldn't bear to think of what Brand must've been through. She wished she'd never begun to doubt him. She'd *known* he was alive. She'd known something had kept him from coming home...but this was horrible.

"Thank you."

His hands cradling her face were gentle, and she kissed the tips of his fingers. Brand gave a little groan.

"How could you think there was someone else? From the day we met there has been no one else. No one. There is only you." His eyes glittered and he leaned forward and covered her lips with his.

Clea half expected the kiss to be dominated by passion. It wasn't. It started off with gentle slowness, with a brush of his lips on hers. Another brush, lingering a little longer. It was only when her lips parted that he seized the moment, his tongue sinking past the soft barrier of her lips and his arms coming around her.

For a few seconds she stood still. Then her senses came to life.

Raising herself on tiptoe to meet his kiss, she let her hands uncurl and her arms creep up, her fingertips skittering across his nape. She closed her eyes, savoring the taste and feel of him. Her body melted against his as Brand plundered her mouth, his tongue moving back and forth, sparking the latent heat in the pit of her belly into a roar of flame.

Under her fingertips, his short hair felt like rough velvet. In the past he'd worn his hair long, and when she'd stroked it she'd been reminded of raw silk. She touched the soft stubble again. There was a lot of time to make up for, a lot of bad days to wipe out of Brand's life.

With a hoarse sound he drew her to him. Clea was conscious of his physical arousal, of the hardness against her stomach. She pressed herself closer, glorying in his heat, his strength.

It was Brand who drew away first. "Trust me, there will never be anyone but you."

Air winnowed against the front of her top where a moment before his body had been plastered. The piercing brightness of Brand's eyes filled her vision. Intent. Honest. Direct. There was no darkness…no distance.

She nodded.

In the back of her mind, echoed the sound of his voice. *All I ever wanted was you.*

Something about how the intensity affected her must've shown in her face because Brand murmured, "Let's go home."

The sun glinted on the brass Welcome Home plaque on the front door. Inside a phone was ringing.

Clea keyed the security code into the pad, then Brand pushed open the door before following her in. The phone had died, the house was quiet.

It *was* home. Warm, welcoming and blessedly empty. Curtis didn't work weekends, and Smythe had retreated to his apartment over the garage complex.

In the bedroom upstairs, shafts of afternoon sunlight

turned the air warm and golden. The subtle hint of jasmine in the air made Brand's chest expand with yearning.

Halting beside the large sleigh bed, piled high with pristine white linen and trimmed with lace, he turned his head to see Clea hovering in the doorway, her eyes holding a sudden trace of uncertainty.

"Come here!" Brand opened his arms, and Clea flew into the circle.

"Are you sure?" she asked.

"God, yes!" Smiling down at her, Brand said, "I never forgot for a minute how beautiful you were." Leaning forward he punctuated the statement with a kiss, then raised his head and caught the sparkles dancing in Clea's eyes.

She started to say something, so he took advantage and kissed her open mouth. Clea fell silent. Cupping her face in his hands as he had beside the lake, he angled his mouth across hers and delved deeper, until his breathing quickened.

At last Brand lifted his head.

Clea's cheeks were flushed.

Brand threaded his fingers through her dark hair, the soft curls twisting between his fingers. *How he had longed for this.* Untangling his fingers, he moved his hands along her back in a lazy, sensual caress until he reached the ruffled edge of her top.

"I want to look at you—all of you."

Clea shimmied out of his embrace. "You first."

For a moment she thought Brand was going to object, then he gave a slow, sexy grin.

"Whatever the lady wants."

Whatever she wanted? Clea gulped. This was supposed to be for him.

Then she watched, dry-mouthed, as he yanked the shirt

they'd shopped for—had it only been this morning?—
loose from his pants, and impatiently fumbled to pull it
up.

With the shirt off, his muscled torso gleamed in the
dazzling afternoon light. Tanned by the desert sun,
she surmised. For a moment, she thought about what
he must've endured, but the grin Brand gave her as he
shucked off his new jeans and the boxers underneath held
enough want and wickedness to eradicate all thought.

Clea's heartbeat picked up.

Shaken by more hunger than she could ever remember
experiencing, she whispered, "Let me help."

He groaned. "Turn around."

"Turn around?" But she was already complying.

The rasp of the zipper was shockingly loud. Clea felt her
top give. Then his lips were against the sensitive skin at
the back of her neck, tracing a line of fire along the erotic
spot only Brand knew about. She shuddered in mindless
delight.

She'd missed this…she'd missed *him*.

He spun her around in his arms and murmured, "You
can help by getting rid of that blasted top. I'm likely to
wreck it right now—and it's too beautiful to be a casualty
to my desperation."

Her hands went to the hem and she eased it up, over
her head, leaving her breasts covered only by the flimsiest
bra.

"Damn, you're beautiful."

Brand drank her in with thirsty eyes.

The bra was a wisp of pale yellow lace, cupping breasts
that were full and voluptuous, the nipples darker than
he remembered. He bit back a groan. Reaching out, he
caressed the curves of her shoulders, her rib cage, her

waist…all the way down to her hips with hands that trembled.

At her hip, his fingers tugged clumsily at the zipper and the skirt dropped into a crumpled heap on the floor. Brand scooped her off her feet, and Clea gave a shriek of surprise. Holding her close to his chest, acutely aware of how scantily clad she was, he made for the endless stretch of bed and gently laid her down.

Naked, he sank down on the bed beside her. Propping himself up on one elbow, he leaned over Clea and nuzzled the curve of flesh that spilled over the top of the lace.

Her skin was soft beneath his lips, and under the delicate lace he could see the dark flesh of the nipple hardening, forming a pointed peak.

His hands shook as he dealt with the clasp at the front of her bra. Once loosened, the scraps of lace fell away. Cupping her breasts, he ran his thumb gently across the swollen tips.

Clea tilted her head back and moaned. Brand leaned forward and replaced his right thumb with his mouth and sucked gently, until her moans grew louder.

His mouth trailed down the side of one breast, planting kisses in the valley between then ascending the other, all the way to the crown.

This time Clea was ready for the wild, sweet sensation. Yet still she couldn't stop the hoarse sound that broke from her throat.

"I'm fighting for restraint," he muttered as he drew her to the edge of the bed, slipping off the last garment separating them, and parting her legs. Brand moved forward into the space he'd created between her thighs. "But I promise I'll take it real slow. I'll be careful. You tell me what you want."

"I'm only pregnant, so I'm hardly likely to break. But

if you want to know, I want you," she murmured taking his head between her hands. "Inside me. Now."

As he moved forward, the light flickered along his tanned limbs, burnishing his skin to the color of polished bronze. Halting, he positioned himself at the entrance to her body.

"Are you sure?" he whispered. "You don't want to wait, to play a little more?"

"There'll be plenty of time to play later. Right now I'm hungry."

"I'm starved, too," he admitted. And, leaning on his elbows, he lightly licked her sensitive lower lip before settling his mouth across hers. Minutes later, he said huskily, "That's just an appetizer."

Her heart thudding with desire, Clea responded through well-kissed lips, "I need a meal."

Brand choked on a burst of laughter. "I've already fed you, insatiable woman!"

It was the first time she'd heard him express such unrestrained joy since his return. It acted as the headiest of aphrodisiacs. She undulated against him, until she felt the pounding of his heart against hers.

When Brand eased one hand between their bodies, she jerked under the stroke of his fingers. Then the touch relaxed, only to be replaced by a familiar blunt warmth.

Clea held her breath. Pushing forward, he slid into her with an ease she hadn't expected.

"Tell me if it hurts."

"It won't hurt," she whispered against the side of his face, relishing the scrape of his jaw on her skin.

They moved in unison, like an unforgotten dance. An intimate dance for lovers. The pace grew quicker, the thrusts of Brand's body deeper. Pleasure twisted, tightening in Clea's body. Until, with a final thrust into her, the release came, sending them both spinning into a realm of color and blinding delight.

Eleven

In the early hours before dawn, Brand woke, hot and sweating, gripped in the clutches of a vivid nightmare. Ugly visions of violence played through his consciousness, and he reached for Clea, pulling her close.

She wriggled beside him with a sleepy sigh, her back spooned to his torso. He kissed her nape and she arched against him like a cat. His body leaped instantly to life.

This time their passion was less playful. It held a fierce and relentless edge. Afterward, Brand wound his arms around her and pulled her up against his body, his eyes drifting shut. Under the hand that rested on her belly something moved.

Brand started, shocked, his mind reeling in turmoil. A baby. A family. *His* family…

In his embrace Clea shifted in her sleep, murmuring restlessly before her breathing settled into a regular rhythm.

But it was a long time before sleep claimed him.

Brand was wakened by a woodpecker drumming in the chestnut tree outside the window.

Beside him, Clea didn't stir.

Turning on his side, he propped himself up on an elbow and watched her as the day brightened. At last her eyes opened, and in the early morning light he caught the first flare of surprise. There was joy, too. And something more...

Clea stared back at him.

Then, before he could gather his defenses, she blurted out, "In the night...you woke me. I felt you touch my stomach." She rolled toward him, reaching for him. "Brand, you need to know, it's not Harry's baby."

Brand shuddered. He didn't want to talk about anything that might bring discord—not after the closeness they'd shared last night. "I will never delve into the circumstances of your baby's conception. I can understand how it might have happened. You must've been lonely."

"Wait!"

Clea bounded out of the bed. Brand couldn't stop himself from admiring the beauty of her naked curves, the fluidity with which she appeared to float rather than walk.

Across the bedroom, she flung open the closet doors. Seconds later Brand heard the safe open with a ping. She drew out a manila folder and opened it. With a single piece of paper in her hand, she came toward him.

Settling back on the bed, she handed it to him then pulled the covers around her nakedness.

Brand's body twisted. "I don't need—"

"Yes, you do."

He glanced down at the black-and-white print, and his signature, a blur at the bottom.

"What's this got to—"

"Look at it!"

He took it from her and then scanned the header, *Client Depositor Storage Agreement.* As he processed the possibilities, he lifted his disbelieving gaze to hers. As from a distance he heard himself saying, "What are you trying to tell me?"

"*You* are my baby's father."

"Impossible." But he could hear the lack of conviction in his own voice. He waved the agreement. "Where did you get this?"

"I found it among the papers in your study when I was going through them—" she swallowed "—last year after I got your ring. I knew the time had come to finalize… things."

"Jesus."

It was a scenario he'd never contemplated.

"Finding it then seemed so right." Clea made a little movement and the covers fell back from her shoulders, exposing pale, creamy skin. "As if it was meant to be. It gave me a purpose to the helplessness I was experiencing. And I was one of the lucky ones—I conceived immediately."

Years ago when he'd first considered storing his sperm, it had seemed fatalistic. A death wish. Yet, some part of him had cautioned that it had little to do with death—and everything to do with life. He could not exclude the likelihood that he might serve in a region where chemical warfare might affect his future health. It had been insurance…for a future. Just in case.

But this…

This—he couldn't take it in.

"You're going to have to let me absorb this," he said at last.

With a small sigh she said, "Blind faith never was your style. And of course you'll want me to undergo paternity testing—I'll find the documentation for the IVF for you, as well. Later. But now, if you'll excuse me, I'm going to take a shower."

Steam billowed through the bathroom in great white clouds.

Brand squinted through it and headed straight for the shower, where he could make out Clea's pale shape through the spray. Without hesitation, he stepped into the tiled cubicle.

The green eyes she raised to his were bright with tears.

"Don't cry!" Brand closed the space between them and wrapped his arms around her sudsy body as the water beat down on them. Bending his head, he could smell the sweet, elusive jasmine that clung to her.

"I'm not crying," she snuffled against his chest.

"You could've fooled me."

She lifted her face. "Brand, I lost my ring—"

It was the last thing he'd expected. Clearly it had upset her immensely. But losing it explained why it wasn't on her finger. "Shh. I'll get you another one."

"It won't be the same." She gave a heartbreaking sob. "I took it off to wash my hands and left it in the ladies' room at the museum. When I went back, it was gone."

He didn't allow her to get another word in. He claimed her mouth. Tasted her tears. And his own eyes grew moist. Shutting them tightly, he kissed her deeper, then lifted his mouth—to draw a breath—before resuming to plant a row of desperate kisses along her lips. Finally, he whispered, "Clea!"

She tilted her head back and water streamed over her cheeks, washing away the tears. "Yes?"

He looked deep into her eyes. "You should stop me. Say something. You want to talk. Remember?"

"I find I need this more." She placed a finger on his lips, silencing him.

At her touch, Brand groaned against her fingertip. "Clea, you finish me."

"I haven't even started," she whispered, drawing the tip of her finger across his bottom lip.

"Stop!"

But Clea only raised herself onto tiptoe, her eyes so close, Brand could see the flecks of gold that made the green sparkle with luminous intensity.

"Before—" he hesitated "—before you regret not talking more first."

"I won't regret this," she assured him, her wet fingers smoothing the hollows below his cheekbones. "We can talk later. You've lost weight. Your cheeks never used to be so defined. But I have to admit that I like the look. Incredibly sexy. Makes you look lean and hungry."

He gave a growl.

Clea laughed.

And, with a surge of yearning, Brand knew this was what he'd longed for during the hot, dry, dark nights more than anything on earth. He loved this woman...with all his heart.

Clea.

He didn't know whether he spoke her name out loud. Or not. All he knew was that she was melting against him, soft and pliant and so very feminine.

"We should—"

"Go to the bedroom?" Brand groaned inwardly at the idea of waiting another minute.

She clung to him.

"You want to make love here? In the shower?" But first

he had to tell her that he believed her. Before he touched her again in a way that would bind them together forever. With tenderness. With reverence. With love.

His distrust…he'd been wrong. Horribly wrong.

He had to make that up to her.

"I can't stop thinking…" Brand palmed her sleek, wet stomach. The curve had grown since that first time he'd recoiled from the shape of the baby the night of the exhibition opening. "About the baby."

"And?" Her hands fell away from his face. Her body had gone stiff, her eyes wide and dark as she waited for his reaction.

With fear? Contempt for himself surged through Brand. "Don't look like that!"

Cupping her stomach with both hands, he moved his attention from her face to the new life that lay between his hands.

His child…

Clea's stomach rose and fell, revealing her emotional reaction to his touch.

"I believe you."

Her mouth rounded in surprise. "You accept that my child is yours?"

He stroked her belly with his fingertips, feeling the solid roundness that could only be the baby's head. There was a ripple of movement under his hands. Brand's heart lurched.

Driven, he lifted his head to meet Clea's wary eyes.

"I think we both know I'm too analytical, too much of a skeptic to ever have accepted the baby without a reasonable explanation." He didn't pause as she opened her mouth to speak. "But I'm not going to demand DNA tests or reports about the IVF—you deserve better. My trust. For me to believe you for no other reason than because you tell me it is so."

Her indrawn breath whistled between them. "It is. And as your wife, your widow, there was no problem with retrieving...the deposit."

Beneath his hands the baby moved. A sense of wonder filled Brand. "I *know* this is my baby."

He slid his hands down, over her bottom, and hoisted her off her feet into his arms, ignoring her squawk of objection. Reaching out, he shut off the water. "Enough talk. Time to carry you over the threshold back into our bedroom."

When Brand finally strolled into the breakfast room on Monday morning, everything appeared more vivid.

Everything had been brightened by the news that he was going to be a father...he and Clea were having a baby. His baby.

His life had changed forever.

In the garden, summer flowers made bold splashes of color, and he blinked against the gold rays slanting through the open French doors. The round table was covered with a stylish tablecloth printed with sunflowers and laid for one. There was no sign of Clea. Brand hadn't expected her to still be here—according to his newly acquired cell phone, it was almost nine. Yet, as on every other morning, she'd been his first thought.

But today it was different. *The baby Clea carried was his.*

He reached out a hand to capture the closest sunbeam. It danced over his fingers, untrapped. *No matter.* He'd awakened for years in a darkened hellhole; he'd never take sunshine for granted again.

Clea.

Drawing his cell phone out of his pocket, he called her number. She answered instantly, and her voice lilted when she heard his voice, causing Brand considerable satisfaction.

"Have dinner with me tonight?" he said huskily, his heartbeat picking up as he waited for her response.

"That would be lovely. Oh, hang on." Brand heard Clea talking to someone in the background. "Brand, I have to go. Alan says the TV crews have arrived to interview us. The Museum Mile Festival is so close everything's happening at once around here. I can't talk now. I'll see you later."

"Good," he purred. "I'll meet you at the museum at five."

"I should come home and change first."

That made him laugh. "Clea, you will look beautiful whatever you wear."

"Thank you." There was a note in her voice that brought a smile to his face. "In that case, I'll see you at five."

As he set the phone down, Brand saw there were messages. He replayed them. One, in particular, piqued his interest.

When Curtis arrived with a pile of blueberry pancakes, Brand had taken note of the place and time to meet his contact. Finally, with the messages played, he picked up his fork and started to eat.

"I've been calling you all weekend."

Clea glanced up from checking the final proof of the glossy Museum Mile Festival program to find Harry standing inside the door of her office.

"I left messages," he continued, aggrieved. "You never called me back."

The weekend had been a magical escape for her and

Brand to discover each other anew. To lay the foundation for their future. But she couldn't possibly explain that to Harry. Instead, Clea said, "I got your messages..." There was an awkward pause. "It's been crazy this morning with the Museum Mile Festival just around the corner," she added lamely.

Harry crossed to stand in front of her desk. "I thought I'd take you to lunch."

Clea pulled a face. "I haven't got time today." Every moment she saved today would go toward escaping to dinner with Brand, Clea thought with a touch of guilt. But she needed to talk to Harry, to tell him there was no need for any charade—Brand knew the truth. Clea glanced at her watch. "I could take a short coffee break downstairs in the courtyard."

"Better than nothing." But Harry looked crestfallen.

"They make a mean pastrami on rye if you want a quick snack," Clea reminded him as she rose from her chair.

Five minutes later they'd found a table in a corner of the busy courtyard beside a planter filled with a riot of summer flowers and shaded by a large green-and-white-striped umbrella. Clea ordered a fruit smoothie while Harry settled for a sandwich and a light beer.

"Isn't this nice?" Clea said when their orders arrived.

Harry was too busy extracting something from his pocket to answer. When he straightened, he said, "I wanted to take you out to lunch to give you this."

This turned out to be a glittering solitaire that had to be at least two carats.

Clea's eyes flew to his face. "I can't accept that, Harry."

"Because Brand came back from the dead?"

There was a note in his voice that caused a chill of dread to feather down her spine. "I can hardly agree to marry you while I'm still married to someone else."

"You were happy to pretend you were going to marry me before."

"It was a stupid stunt to pull—unfair to both you and Brand."

And unworthy of her.

In that first blood-rush when she'd told Brand she was going to marry Harry, she'd wanted to wound him. She'd reacted badly. Retaliating for the bewilderment and loss she'd experienced when he disappeared. Punishing him for devastating her with his distrust when he'd discovered that she was pregnant. The truth was she'd been so angry with Brand that she'd wanted to let him know that even if he couldn't love her, didn't want her, there were other men out there who felt differently. It had been all about her anger—and her damn pride.

Clea sighed. "I should *never* have embroiled you in it."

Harry sat forward in his seat. "Divorce Brand—marry me. I'll always be there for you. And I wouldn't go MIA on you. It would be good. We'd share what we've always shared, and I'd give your baby a father. We can make this work."

Without waiting for an answer, he reached for her hand and slid the ring onto her finger, into the empty groove where Brand's ring had sat until she'd removed…and lost…it.

The solitaire felt tight and uncomfortable—and just plain *wrong*.

"No!" Clea started to tug it off, only to have Harry's hands close over hers.

His hazel eyes were solemn. "I bought that ring for you weeks ago—before your husband turned up. I want you to divorce Brand. I want to marry you. Clea, I love you—I've always loved you."

Clea stared at Harry aghast. She glanced surreptitiously

around to see if anyone had overheard. But fortunately no one was paying any attention to their table tucked away in the corner.

Moving her gaze back to Harry, Clea settled for, "I never knew."

How could she have been so blind?

Harry gave her a wry smile. "I dreamed someday you would look at me and know that I was the only man for you."

"Oh, Harry..."

How could she have been so insensitive? All those years she'd treated him like a brother, like a friend. How he must've suffered. She'd fallen in love with Brand...and left Harry to break the news of her Vegas wedding to her father. Clea closed her eyes and drew a deep breath.

Then she'd told Brand she was marrying Harry...

For the first time in her life she actively disliked herself.

Opening her eyes, she turned her hands over and laced her fingers through his. "I'm so sorry. How selfish you must think me."

"You don't love me?"

Clea shook her head slowly. "Not the way you deserve to be loved. I wish I did." She gave his fingers a gentle squeeze before releasing them and drew the ring off her finger. "I can't wear this."

The tight, brave smile Harry gave her as he took his ring back almost broke her heart.

"What we have could be very good—I've known you your whole life."

"Harry—"

"Don't be too hasty, Clea." He paused, and she glimpsed the first glitter of annoyance in his eyes. It was gone so quickly she decided she must've imagined it. "If you're holding out for Brand, you're making a mistake."

Clea swallowed her instinctive objection and lowered her lashes. Harry was hurting, she told herself. It was to be expected that he'd attack Brand.

"Brand is my baby's father," she said at last.

"He's a cold, dangerous bastard."

Snapshots of the weekend flashed through her mind. Brand's gentleness…his joy…his tears. Harry didn't know Brand or he wouldn't make such an absurd claim.

"Think about how much more we would share. Your father would be delighted—and mine would be dancing in his grave. Two dynasties merging."

"Dynasties?" The grandiose term alerted Clea. "Is this about money? Please tell me the rumor you're in financial trouble isn't true."

"Who told you that?"

The red rising up Harry's neck told her that Brand had been right.

"Why didn't *you* tell me? I could've helped you with a loan to tide you over."

He smiled ruefully. "Oh, Clea. It wouldn't have made a dent."

Suddenly Clea didn't feel like finishing her smoothie. Pushing the tall glass away, she said quietly, "I could've asked Dad to help."

"Your father knows. If you married me—" he glanced down at her tummy, which was starting to show "—and we raised your son together, he was prepared to settle my debts."

Shock rippled through her. "My father said that?"

"Your father likes me—he's always wanted us to get married."

Harry's claim rang true. Yet offering to pay Harry to marry her…

"Don't look at me like that Clea." There was an

undercurrent of impatience in Harry's voice. "It makes perfect sense for you to marry me—it always did."

Had her father...and Harry...been so sure of her? Had they believed she would marry Harry eventually, even though she didn't love him?

A sharp blade of betrayal stabbed Clea. Opening her purse she extracted a $50 bill and set it down on the table to cover the meal, then she rose to her feet.

Even as Harry started to bluster, she shook her head and said simply, "Goodbye, Harry."

Twelve

At five o'clock Clea found Brand in the long gallery, examining her tiger. Clad in a new Cesare Attolini suit, he stood unmoving as Clea came up behind him, her heels clicking on the marble floor.

Halting beside him, Clea cast him a sideways glance, and her stomach dropped like an elevator as she took in the reality of the man. The white shirt with a darker stripe and an immaculately knotted tie drew attention to Brand's smoothly shaved, tanned jawline. "He's gorgeous, don't you think?"

And she wasn't only speaking of the stone tiger.

"A relic from another time." Brand was engrossed. "He's fierce and splendid, with a regal dignity."

"Noble, isn't he?" Clea's lips curled up at the pun.

Brand tipped his head to one side. "Yes." He fell silent, clearly captivated by the creature that had been crafted with care by a pair of hands thousands of years ago.

"Sometimes I wonder if it wouldn't be simpler living in his world," said Clea. "What's to worry about? Besides sourcing food and water, finding a mate to ensure that he passed his genes onto cubs, then going his own way again."

Brand slanted her a very male glance. "Straightforward instincts—sex, survival, hunger, thirst."

Clea grinned. "Exactly!"

"All kills done for food." Brand's voice dropped. "No need to consider greed, lies and deception."

He'd lost her. Her smile faded. "What do you mean?"

Was he referring to her lie about her engagement to Harry? Or leading him to believe the baby was Harry's? Ever since seeing Harry earlier, a sick feeling had swirled in the pit of her stomach. Regret. Guilt.

Brand shrugged, his shoulders rising and falling under the suit jacket. He turned his head and she caught a flash of white as he grinned. "Nothing. Just empty philosophizing."

And Clea melted with relief.

When Brand's gaze swept over her, causing tingles of awareness to flood her, she was glad she'd worn the sea-green chiffon shift for the scheduled TV interview she'd had that morning—she knew she looked good.

Then his eyes rested on the curve of her baby bump. And when his eyes returned to her again, his expression was indescribable.

"I always knew you were beautiful—but now you glow."

His soft words pushed the smoldering coals of the lunchtime conversation with Harry from her mind as she counted her blessings. Brand was back. Their baby was growing. They would finally be a family.

She linked an arm through Brand's, tugging him toward the exit. "Where are we going for dinner?"

"Not far. I played it safe and booked a table at Fives on Fifth Avenue."

"The food there is always splendid."

Casting a last look over her shoulder at the tiger, Clea searched the proud head and solid form for a hint of what had inspired Brand to make that enigmatic statement about greed and deception. All she saw was a splendid, heroic animal she'd spent countless hours admiring—and no sign of the darkness to which Brand had alluded.

Yet Clea knew better than to ask Brand what he'd meant. She had to trust him to tell her when he was ready.

Fives had a welcoming ambience. The spacious room with its carefully arranged tables provided the perfect degree of privacy.

Yet, despite the easy conversation between them, Brand knew something was troubling Clea. After devouring the last of the beef tenderloin, he asked, "What's the matter?"

Clea neatly set her knife and fork down. "You were right."

Patiently, he waited as she chose her words.

"As you said, Harry is in financial trouble. He thought I would divorce you—and marry him."

Electrifying tension tightened Brand's muscles. "That's never going to happen."

Clea gave a half laugh. "I know. I told Harry so."

Brand counted to ten as the waiter removed their empty dinner plates and amazed himself by his feeling of utter cool. "What did he say?"

"He tried to make me believe that he loved me."

The pain in Clea's voice twisted Brand's gut inside out. A moment of truth faced him. It was hard for him to vocalize what he'd rather have kept hidden. But Clea deserved more. "I suspect that he does love you. My return, causing him to lose you again, would've hammered it home to him."

But she was already shaking her head. "I was never his to lose. No, he was simply prettying up a mercenary proposal. If he married me, my father would have bailed him out of debt."

Clea looked so forlorn that, uncaring of the attention he might draw from other diners, Brand got to his feet and went around the table to crouch down beside her chair. Putting an arm around her, he hugged her clumsily. Clea dropped the paper napkin she'd already shredded and threw her arms around his shoulders.

Brand rested his cheek against hers. "Never in this lifetime will I let that happen."

This was *his* woman, and she was carrying *his* child. The surge of primitive possessiveness took him aback. Hell, he regretted not flattening Hall-Lewis when he had the chance. The man had wounded Clea.

"Harry is an idiot," he said softly.

To Brand the woman in his arms was worth far more than a monetary fortune.

Clea leaned against him. "I feel like I've totally misjudged him. He was my friend—my best friend."

"I'm sure he thinks he still is your friend."

"Then how can he do this to me?"

"Harry will always love himself most. Consider him a shallow idiot." Brand turned his head and pressed a kiss onto her cheek. "Money makes men do the stupidest things…"

Clea sniffed then laughed. She tilted her head to one side, and considered him. "But not you."

It was uttered with confidence.

Brand shook his head, and, still hunkered down beside her, stroked a curl off her cheek, relieved that her eyes had lost that forsaken look. "I learned a long time ago there are more important things in life than money."

The sentiment came from the heart. The past four years had only served to underscore his belief. Health. Sanity. Love. None of those could be bought...

She sniffed again and dropped her forehead until it met his. "I just feel so..." Her voice wobbled.

Betrayed.

The notion caused an ache deep in his chest. His anger at Hall-Lewis intensified. No one knew better in the world what she was going through than Brand. He closed his eyes and hugged her to him, trying to absorb her heartbreak.

"Thank you for not saying *I told you so,*" she murmured, her breath mingling with his.

"I only wish I could've saved you the experience of being hurt by Harry."

"I'll get over it," she said. "At least I have you—so there's a place in my heart that is intact. My pride is smarting right now. I feel so foolish. Why do I always trust the wrong people?"

With a sigh Clea sat up, and Brand's arms fell away. He rose slowly to his feet.

He'd betrayed her trust, too.

It wasn't a pleasant realization. He had no wish to be lumped on a list with people who had let Clea down.

He'd much rather be the person she trusted above all others. The person she turned to in the darkness of night. To protect her from the nightmares, the monsters, the heartbreak.

Sliding back into his chair, he asked, "Would you like dessert?"

Clea shook her head.

"Coffee?"

"Cancel coffee." She gave him a long look. "You know

what? The meal was delicious, but now I'd like to go home."

Home.

They were in agreement on that. Brand knew there was no place else he wanted to be.

For Clea, the days that followed slipped past in a haze.

She worked nonstop on preparing the new exhibition for the Museum Mile Festival, and when she came home at night she was dead tired. The pregnancy had also finally started to show, and she was favoring looser dresses that were well suited to the New York summer.

Their time together had settled into a routine. Often, in the evenings, she and Brand would prepare dinner and they'd eat it out on the deck overlooking the garden. Later, Brand would draw her a warm bath, and afterward he rubbed her back…and anything else that ached. He would rub cream into the stretching skin of her stomach—he was fascinated by the baby moving.

And frequently they made love.

On the weekends, they decorated the nursery. Brand had painted the walls himself in a pale leaf-green that echoed the garden outside. And they were busy furnishing the room with pieces selected with love and care.

Clea knew that his days, too, were full. Brand had leased new office space, and tempted Karen, his trusty PA, to return to work for him. Clea had visited the offices and was stunned by how much her husband had achieved in so little time.

He often attended meetings she knew little about. While she knew he was receiving counseling to come to terms with his imprisonment, there were times when she worried that he might be returning to his old ways of secrecy that had caused such distance and misunderstandings in the past.

But she had promised to give Brand time. He'd suffered terrible trauma, the very least she could do was offer understanding.

He would talk when he'd worked everything through for himself. After four years, Clea had thought she'd mastered her impatience. She was wrong. She'd never been more impatient than she was now. It was difficult...the hardest thing she'd done in her life. She wanted to talk, to know what he was thinking, how he was dealing with what had happened to him in the time they'd been apart. She itched to climb inside his head...feel what he was thinking. But pressure...impatience...wasn't what he needed from her.

It was tough to wait. But he'd asked her to trust him on this. And she had to respect his request.

Almost three weeks had passed since he had come home, and Brand found he was still entering the house each evening filled with anticipation at seeing Clea.

Tonight, after a meeting with a shadowy ex-special forces operative, he was later than usual. Curtis had already left. Clea was not out on the deck admiring the garden. Nor was she curled up on the chesterfield in the study. Brand took the stairs two at a time.

He found her in the nursery beside the crib they'd purchased together a few days earlier, securing a mobile made of yellow ducks overhead. She hadn't heard him arrive, and Brand paused in the doorway, taking in the picture she made in a pair of faded jeans, a white T-shirt and bare feet, before committing it to memory.

Given the questions he'd been asking for the past few weeks, Brand risked unleashing the phantom monsters buried deep in his unconscious mind—monsters he suspected would never be contained once they'd escaped.

But he needed answers. Only then would he be able to regain the peace and sanity he craved. Only then could he get on with his life with Clea.

He shifted slightly on his feet, and Clea turned her head. Instantly her face lit up with a smile of delight.

"Brand! I knew you'd be home any minute."

Her pleasure warmed him, melting the cold emptiness inside.

He went toward her then, took her in his arms and nuzzled the soft patch at the side of her neck above the neckline of the cotton shirt.

She giggled. "That tickles." She hooked her fingers into the waistband of his suit pants. "I have something for you."

"All I need is you."

It was true. She was his sunshine…his love…his everything. And his greatest fear was that finding the answers he sought might only hurt Clea more.

Reluctantly, he released her. She darted out through the nursery door and he followed as she ran down the stairs and then disappeared into his study.

By the time he caught up with her, she was hovering beside his desk. He'd always loved the satin finish of the carved rosewood, but today his gaze landed on the small black box resting on the blotter.

"What is it?"

"Open it."

The box fitted easily into his palm. He lifted the lid and his breath hissed out when he saw what lay within.

His wedding ring.

There was a luminous glow in her eyes. "I thought you might want to wear it again."

"I do."

I do. It was a refrain of their vows, a moment engraved forever in his memory.

"Here." Clea reached past him and took the ring out of the box. "Give me your hand."

Emotion closed his throat as he watched the band of gold slide onto his finger.

"And don't ever take it off!"

His eyes jumped to hers. "Not of my free will."

Last time it had been ripped off. Brand had fought so hard not to give it up that he'd been beaten for his resistance.

Clea released his hands. "You have no idea of the despair the return of your ring caused me."

At the back of his mind, something nagged.

Leaning against the desk, Brand folded his arms across his chest and asked carefully, "Who returned it?"

"It was turned in last year for a reward. By a money-lender living in a desert village not far from Baghdad, close to the scene of the crash that supposedly took your life. He must have had it for years. I was lucky it never sold."

Brand homed in on the detail that interested him the most. "The scene of the crash?"

"Of the SUV you rented."

"Clea, I've never had an accident in a vehicle I rented."

Brand thought back to his kidnapping. He'd been snatched by four gunmen off the streets of Baghdad, nowhere near the desert. The darkness of the void he was facing widened.

"But the investigator I hired reported that you'd rented a vehicle in Kuwait to get into Baghdad," she protested, coming closer, her face puzzled.

"I did rent a vehicle," he said patiently, "but I certainly never crashed it."

"But…" Clea's voice faded. "I don't understand."

Nor did he. Yet. Clearly the conversation was upsetting her, but he needed details if he was ever to make sense of the events that had devastated his—their—lives. He changed tack. "Didn't it occur to you that I might not have been in the vehicle at the time?"

"Of course! I asked for proof. I was told that your burned remains had been buried in a mass grave. That what was left of you couldn't be located to ship home."

The horror in her voice was unfeigned. Brand steeled himself not to be swayed by it. "That information was clearly wrong."

Her breathing was ragged beside him, her distress palpable. She touched his forearm, and he noticed that her fingers were trembling.

"I know that…now. I wouldn't have had you declared dead on that basis alone—at first I refused to accept that you were dead. But the ring changed everything. I knew you must be dead." The pain in her eyes hurt him.

"You didn't consider that I might've taken my ring off and disposed of it for cash?"

She shook her head, her expression fierce. "Never. Everyone tried to tell me you'd walked out on our marriage—I refused to believe it. Even when I was shown photos of you at a café in Athens with Anita and told you'd been sighted with her in Baghdad, too, I trusted you."

"I'd hired Anita as a consultant to check into artifacts I was interested in."

"I *told* Harry—Dad—everyone—that she was a colleague…not your lover. That she must've been helping you establish whether a prospective purchase was fake—or checking out its provenance."

He hadn't retained Anita to research an artifact he planned to buy, but that was not relevant now. It sank in that Clea had been through living hell, and through it all she'd believed in him. She'd been loyal…faithful.

Yet he'd doubted her on his first night back. His own hurt and the overpowering sense of betrayal over her pregnancy had caused him to stonewall her demands for an explanation of where he'd been. And why. Then the puzzle of why he'd been kidnapped had taken over; and discussing his sinister theories with her had been out of the question.

Now discomfort settled heavily in his belly. Perhaps Clea was right. Blind faith had never been his style. His special forces training had only reinforced the idea that trust was the currency of the weak and gullible. Over the years skepticism and distrust had become second nature to him, creating a cool distance that allowed him to calculate…then act with greater effectiveness.

Trust was far from easy…and Clea was far better at it than he. His distrust was still alive and kicking. Brand weighed how the ring had gotten from Akam to a moneylender many miles away. And who might have photographed him and Anita together…for what purpose… and whether there had ever been a wreck in the desert as Clea so clearly believed. Or whether paranoia had finally set in for good.

Through it all, Akam's claim that he'd been hired to kill Brand rang through his head, adding to his growing disquiet.

"Then, if you weren't captured after the crash, what happened?" Clea's question broke his focus. "How did you come to be imprisoned?"

Keeping all emotion out his voice, Brand said, "I was kidnapped off the streets of Baghdad, nowhere near the desert, early one evening."

"Kidnapped in the city?" Clea gripped his upper

arms. "That doesn't sound random—it suggests you were targeted"

"So it would appear." That was the riddle that plagued him in the darkest night. The question he had never wanted to answer. Unfolding his arms, he hooked them around her shoulders and drew her to his chest. It was easier not to look at her. To stroke her back, feel the warm softness of her body pressed against his. "But my captors were smugglers—no less dangerous, but not your typical hired guns. Later I was told they'd had orders to kill me." Despite the sound of Clea's sharp indrawn breath, he plowed on. "But Akam, the leader of the group, is a distrustful bastard. He decided to keep me alive as insurance…he was paranoid about being double-crossed. From some of the dissension that followed, I gathered that payment had become a problem. I suspect Akam thought I might be worth more to him as a ransom victim, but as time passed, that proved to have been a risky error in judgment. A price had been put on his own head, so saving his skin and keeping out of sight became more of a priority than ransoming me. In the end, as I told you before, it was Akam who let me go and arranged for me to get out of Iraq—for a tidy sum, of course, which I have now paid. But worth every cent."

Within the circle of his arms, Clea was trembling. Brand tightened his hold, then let his arms fall away as she shifted restlessly.

She leaned back and inspected his face. "So who wanted you dead?"

"I don't know yet," said Brand grimly, though he had his suspicions. "But I will find out."

Clea had taken his hand, was holding onto it, as though she would never let go. "The investigators even had a photo of a mangled wreck in your file—it made me die a little inside every time I looked at it."

Brand clasped his free hand over their joined hands in comfort. "I'm here."

"Was it totally fake? Or *did* a man and woman die out there in the desert?"

That surprised him. "A man and a *woman?*"

"Supposedly you and Anita."

Brand fell silent.

"Have you been in touch with Anita since your return?"

Brand sensed her tension as she waited for his answer. "No. Maybe it's time I talked to your investigators. How did you find them?"

"My father. He knew of them from Harry, who'd used them in the course of his import-export business." Her eyes widened. "You don't really think that Anita might have…?" The question trailed away and her grip on his hand tightened convulsively.

"I don't know." But he couldn't stop the fury that ignited at Hall-Lewis's involvement. Again. "After I've spoken to those investigators, I suspect I'll have to go away for a few days to do some checking."

"You're going back to Baghdad?"

There was naked fear in her eyes.

"It may not come to that." He kissed the top of her head, then freed his hand from her hold and cupped her stomach. "You need to look after junior. I'll be gone for a week at most—I'll make sure I'm back for the Museum Mile Festival. And this time, my ring will not leave my hand. I promise."

Clea couldn't halt the creep of dread that suffused her after Brand's departure. Even though he spoke to her each night, she longed for him to put the past behind him. She worried, too, about the burgeoning fear that Harry had played a part in his disappearance. It would be another betrayal by the man she'd considered her best friend for so long. And it would forever change her life.

Despite Brand's promise that he would return, she couldn't contain the writhing fear that this time he might not come back.

At least there was plenty to keep her busy as the final preparations for the Museum Mile Festival got underway. Determined to continue with her day-to-day life, Clea shopped for a birthday present for her dad, and, in an instant of impulsivity, she got a book on parenting for Brand. A visit to her doctor for a checkup reassured her that the baby was progressing well—and in her spare moments she continued decorating the nursery.

Before Brand left, he'd told her that he'd learned little of significance from the investigators, but he had confirmed through other contacts that Anita had disappeared around the same time he had. Did his departure indicate more than concern for a missing colleague? She forced herself to dismiss the little green monster whispering in her ear.

She was no longer the same naive, newly married young bride he'd left behind four years ago. This time she was a woman. A woman who had experienced loss... and betrayal.

This time it was not easy to ignore her misgivings.

But she loved Brand, and he'd vowed to return. She had to trust him to do so because, without trust, her love was nothing but an empty promise.

Thirteen

The Museum Mile Festival was in full swing by the time Clea received Brand's call to let her know he was back. It was already past noon, and she'd just been starting to think he wouldn't make it.

Her heart soared.

All the way along Fifth Avenue, the crowds were in a celebratory mood. With the road blocked off and bands playing in the street, Clea found the Mardi Gras atmosphere contagious. So when she saw Brand get out of a cab and eye the long queue still waiting to enter the museum, she hurried out to intercept him.

In his dark Italian suit with a beautifully knotted tie he looked smoothly handsome and urbane. He'd shaved, too, she noticed.

"You've already been home."

"To wash off the travel dust." He swept her up and swung her around, then planted a kiss on her lips. "I missed you," he said after a long moment.

Breathlessness filled her. "I should've given you a gate pass," she managed.

He set her down, and she gave him a close look. "Are you okay?"

He nodded. "I'm ready to talk. But first, I want to see what you've done with the Museum Mile Festival."

Her enthusiasm brimmed over. "It's been a fantastic day!" Taking his hand she led him past the line of waiting people, up the stairs to the second floor to the large and airy west wing gallery.

A crowd had formed.

Doing her best to ignore the sizzle that shot up her arm from their intertwined fingers, she said, "Come, there's something I want to show you."

But Brand had stopped to examine a Sumerian clay tablet in a glass case where two young boys were reading the display label. Clea suppressed a smile. Brand had bought the tablet five years ago after a huge amount of work to establish its provenance and ensure that it hadn't been stolen or illegally removed from a dig. It was his reputation for cutting a shrewd deal after exacting scrutiny that had made him one of the most highly paid antiquities importers in the world, and had guaranteed him his first million.

It had taken all Clea's powers of persuasion to convince him that the tablet belonged in a museum. And not just any museum—*this* museum. But Brand had known that by virtue of their marital relationship Clea's integrity would be at risk if he sold the piece to the museum. Instead he'd decided to donate the artifact. His scruples had cost him a tidy sum, but Brand had always said it had been worth it to see the joy on her face.

Dragging Brand away from the tablet, Clea led him to the main display case, and the glorious marble mask inside became visible, and Brand halted. "Where did that come from?"

"The same collection as the vase at the back of the gallery. I call the mask the Lady of the Temple. I suspect she must have come from one of Inanna's temples."

"Your father's old friend sold it to the museum?"

A note in Brand's voice made Clea give him a sharp glance. Keeping her tone easy, she said, "That's right."

"I have sometimes thought—rather radically—that all antiquities should stay in the country of their origin. It would make everything far more cut-and-dried."

Clea swung around to face him. "Using that reasoning, the Elgin Marbles should go back to Athens."

He shrugged. "Perhaps they should."

"Brand!"

"It's not heresy." He defended his position. "The Greeks have been after their return forever—just as the Egyptians have sought to recover the Rosetta Stone."

The curator in her said with feeling, "It leaves a huge hole in those collections to have to return such popular artifacts…and think about all the members of the public who would miss out on being inspired to learn more about foreign cultures. Hey, who knows how many museum artifacts have led to visits to other lands?"

"The objects belong in their own countries and their own cultures."

"But there are times when we need to guard treasures for other cultures—treasures that are important for all humanity."

"Guard…not steal," said Brand in a low voice.

"What do you mean by that?"

He raised a dark eyebrow. "You don't know?"

"Stop talking in riddles."

Brand held her gaze for a long, charged moment.

"Either you've become an accomplished liar—which I don't believe—or you're still too naive to be let out on your own."

"I've grown up."

That caused Brand's face to break into a smile, lightening his grave expression. "Don't grow up too much. The wide-eyed ingenue is part of your charm."

Clea didn't know whether to be amused or offended. In the end she chose to persist in trying to get to the bottom of Brand's oblique comment.

"What do you think I'm too naive to grasp?"

Brad was watching her through narrowed eyes. "You don't think it's curious that one collector has so many prize pieces that are undocumented?"

Relief—mixed with rising irritation—swept through her. "They are well-documented and the provenance can be traced back prior to the 1970s. Since when did a legitimately acquired antiquity become theft, Brand?" She gave a snort of impatience. "And where does that leave you? You spent a decade amassing considerable wealth trading antiquities. Would you call every one of those transactions thefts?"

"I worked exceptionally hard to ensure that I never dealt in stolen artifacts and black-market goods, to build a reputation that would withstand scrutiny. You of all people know that. Sure, it made it tough to find legitimate stock, but, as I told you all those years ago when I bought that tablet—" he jerked his thumb in the direction of the display "—it was important to me."

She'd loved his integrity then, but she still couldn't shake the sense that he was accusing her of something. "What are you implying?"

"Ten years ago, when I was on a tour of duty with the SAS, I attended a viewing of never-before-exhibited artifacts in Istanbul. I already knew Anita—she got me an invitation. Some of the items had been sent by the Iraq Museum. There was a truly unique marble mask the likes of which I have never seen before or since—yet now I find the identical twin of that piece here."

It dawned on Clea that Brand was speaking of her Lady of the Temple.

"That's impossible." But her heart was racing. "According to the documentation, the mask has been in the United States for over fifty years."

Foreboding stirred. Brand didn't lie. His reputation was built on knowledge and integrity. And to suggest that the piece was a twin would be ludicrous—especially given the similar situation with the vase that resembled the Vessel of Inanna. Apprehension settled firmly into the pit of her stomach.

"Are you claiming that we bought a stolen artifact? That they were never purchased from my father's friend?" Her hands were clammy against on the fabric of her skirt. "That's a very serious charge to level at the museum." At Alan…and her father.

"Four years ago, Anita and I applied to the Iraq Museum for permission to photograph that mask—and a number of pieces in the same collection. My request was not-so-politely refused." He raised an eyebrow. "Coincidence? I think not."

"Four years ago." Her eyes went wide. "But that's…"

He nodded. "I became curious. I started asking questions. I'd already hired Anita to do some research for me—about a small tablet I'd seen in this museum, which Alan had assured me had sound provenance. It reminded me remarkably of a tablet I'd seen in Istanbul, and that bothered me. The deeper I dug, the more I doubted that the mask had also ever made it back to the Iraq Museum from Istanbul."

Clea was conscious of the weight of his gaze. "Could you confirm whether either the tablet or the mask were ever reported stolen?"

Brand shook his head. "But someone evidently knew I had shown interest in that piece. Someone who knew of the thefts. And that someone meant business."

"What do you mean?" Clea's heart stopped in shock.

"Anita has not been seen since—I suspect she's dead." Brand was speaking softly, his eyes rapidly scanning the gallery as if he feared they might be overheard. "We can discuss this further tonight—after the festivities are over."

"No." Clea tossed her head. She wanted to get to the bottom of this disturbing revelation. "This is too important to delay. Let's go to my office."

Once they were inside her office, Brand closed the door behind them.

Clea crossed to the window where the courtyard teemed with people below. At last, she swung back around to Brand, her face filled with confusion.

Before she could ask the questions that threatened to tumble out, Brand began to talk. "Ever since you mentioned that you were given my ring that's troubled me."

Clea's brow wrinkled into a frown.

"It was a little too convenient, the way in which it turned up as proof when you refused to accept any other explanation." Brand watched her through narrowed eyes. "I was kidnapped almost four years ago. But that ring was forced off my finger only last August."

Gooseflesh broke over her skin. "That would mean…" Her voice trailed away.

"It would mean that all the time someone who could get

that ring into your hands knew what had really happened to me. Certainly someone knew Akam held me captive—it was enough to make him extremely jumpy. It's why he kept me alive, instead of killing me, as he'd been ordered."

"What you're suggesting is impossible," said Clea, aghast.

"Diabolical, yes. Impossible? I'm not so sure." Brand raised his shoulders and let them fall. "But I hope you're right."

Clea tried to speak. Her voice emerged in a shaky croak. "You believe Harry arranged for you to be killed?"

Brand shook his head. "That's what I'd hoped. But when I look at who stands to gain the most, I don't think it's Harry."

"Then who?"

"Your father."

The festival was over.

Brand had left earlier and Clea had convinced herself that he must have it wrong. He'd made a mistake. Her father was not a murderer. Yet doubt lingered. Brand had never lied to her...and he seemed so sure.

The uncertainty was driving her crazy.

When she could bear no more, she called Brand to let him know that she'd be leaving shortly. It took her only a few minutes to unlock the wall safe in her office, and retrieve what she was seeking.

Then she left, locking the door behind her, and made for the underground garage to fetch her car.

The surprise on her father's face twenty minutes later when Clea stepped out of the private elevator into his penthouse apartment was genuine.

"I thought you'd be on your way home, Clea?"

She crossed the exquisite Bokhara rug into the

gadget-filled TV area where her father spent most of his time. He followed, hard on her heels.

"Sit down, I'll pour us each a glass of wine."

"Not for me, thanks." Clea patted her tummy with one hand. "I can't stay long. Dad, where did the investigators find this?"

Donald Tomlinson's expression hardened as she drew a sheaf of photos from the file tucked under her arm and showed him the top one: an image of Brand's wedding ring.

He blustered. "You know the answer to that! A money-lender responded to the Wanted notices we circulated in hopes of locating some of Brand's personal effects."

She drew out a photo of the wreck. "This gave me nightmares for months...years."

Sinking down on the edge of the deep-red leather sofa, her father said, "But we already knew about the car wreck—"

"Brand was never in that crash—and the ring was taken from him a long time later by men who had kidnapped him. Just when I was demanding proof of his death. Isn't that a little coincidental?" Clea started to pray. *Please, God. Let Brand be wrong about her father's involvement.*

Her father didn't respond. His face had turned wooden.

"Dad, you need to tell me. Brand believes you planned to have him killed."

"That's a goddamn lie!"

"Dad!" Her father never swore in the company of women. She retreated a step, the file clutched in front of her.

Donald Tomlinson was on his feet. "Don't back away from me like that. You don't believe it, do you?"

"I...I don't know," she stuttered.

Her father's nostrils flared. "You're not sure? You'd believe him over me?"

Sharp pains splintered through her. Still clutching the file, Clea cradled her belly. "I don't know what—who—to believe anymore. Oh, Daddy, I'm so confused." A sob stuck in her throat.

When he opened his arms, Clea hesitated. He let them drop slowly to his sides. "You believe him."

"Convince me that it's a lie," she begged.

"*Convince* you? I'm your father. Where's your loyalty? Who brought you up? Who was both father and mother to you after that bitch deserted us for another man and his children?"

It was Clea's turn to stare. She'd never seen this bitter, poisonous side of her father.

After a long silence, she mustered every last shred of dignity she possessed. "You've always had my un-questioning loyalty."

Until now.

With every passing moment her unshakable confidence in her father was eroding. "Harry says—"

"What?"

The whiplash question made Clea jump. She swallowed nervously. "Harry told me you knew that the only reason he wanted to marry me was because he's broke."

"That's not true!" Sticking his jaw out, her father said, "Harry has always wanted to marry you—he would've made the perfect husband if that other bastard hadn't interfered."

"I fell in love with Brand."

"Love!"

"At least Brand didn't have to be bribed to marry me." At her father's stunned expression, Clea said recklessly, "Yes, Harry told me you'd offered him a sweetener."

"It's what you should've done all along…it would've made everything right."

Clea's eyes widened. "Is that why you tried to kill Brand? So that I would be free to marry Harry?" It made her stomach roll. "I feel quite sick." She started to turn away. "I should go home."

Her father's low voice stopped her. "You don't understand, Clea. He was going to destroy me—everything I'd built up."

Shocked, she swung back. "What do you mean?"

"The first time you introduced him to me, I knew. Brand is sharper than a knife—he sees things most people don't notice. He's a cold, clever bastard. That analytical brain puts together information and spits out the answer. He'd lived in Iraq and Afghanistan. He understood the antiquities trade in the Middle East—the players, the black market, the legitimate market. To top it all, he had that peculiar gift of being able to recognize a fraud at a glance…and his ability to recall information about the obscurest pieces was formidable. I knew it would only be a matter of time."

Clea's confusion hardened into certainty—and bitter disappointment. She rubbed the nagging pain at her side and it seemed to ease. "You're involved in buying looted artifacts."

Like the Vessel of Inanna. And the Lady of the Temple. And heaven only knew how many other pieces.

"I defended you," she said sadly, "I told Brand you would never be involved in such things." Clea bit her lip, remembering her rage at Brand. How blind her loyalty had been. "I don't know you at all, do I?"

She owed Brand an apology. He was right: She *was* too naive to be let out on her own.

Her father spread his arms out wide. "I tried to spare

you the news of his death, my dear. If you had believed that your husband had deserted you for another woman and divorced him, it would've made it…easier."

"But I never believed that." Clea knew she must be wearing her most mulish expression. "Which meant you needed to come up with another scenario—so you got your 'investigators' to report that Brand had died in a car crash in the desert with his nonexistent lover. Problem was, the men you'd hired to kill him kidnapped him instead—and kept him alive as insurance."

"Harry and I had used them to move antiquities over the border into Turkey before. What I didn't know was that Harry had been shortchanging them. So they took Brand and disappeared, hoping for a bigger payoff somewhere down the line. Until one of the men surfaced with Brand's wedding ring after seeing our poster—he contacted Harry to claim the reward." Her father sighed. "I knew then that we had Brand within reach."

"So you put a contract out on the kidnappers—and their victim. If you'd succeeded I never would have known that you'd tried to have my husband executed."

"Once it started, things snowballed."

But the seeds of doubt about Brand's adultery had been successfully planted and after Brand's return they had flourished. *She'd been so gullible.* Clea felt like bursting into tears. But what would that accomplish?

"Dad—" Donald Tomlinson was still her father "—Brand's seen the Lady of the Temple and he knows where it originally came from. I have no doubt he will go to the FBI."

He walked away, stopping beside a pedestal holding an ancient bronze—Clea didn't even want to contemplate whether that piece, too, had been obtained through illicit means.

"I knew this day would come from the moment I met

that man." He reached out and touched the bronze. "And when your husband came back, I tried to buy time. I tried to talk Alan out of exhibiting the mask—told him we should wait until the museum could display all the pieces together. But he wouldn't—" her father turned to face Clea "—and I couldn't tell him why. It has been like standing frozen in the path of an oncoming train."

"So Alan wasn't in on it?" Clea had wondered. Alan authorized all purchases and checked the provenance of every item.

"He had suspicions, I think. He never asked many questions—as long as some kind of provenance was provided. Enough to cover his bureaucratic ass."

"I never suspected a thing." It was hard to believe. But she'd always looked up to her father...viewed him as omnipotent and honest.

"You're my daughter, my only child. Of course, I never wanted you embroiled in that darker side of my life."

"But you were prepared to let me marry Harry, knowing he was in on it? Didn't you think I might be drawn into it by accident?"

Her father gave her a sad smile. "We planned to stop while we were riding high. Four years ago we were nearing that point. If Brand hadn't started asking questions or gone to Iraq to find answers things might have been different. The mask was going to be our retirement fund."

"Don't blame Brand. And it didn't work out that way— Harry is broke."

"He's developed a gambling problem in the past few years."

That stunned Clea. "Harry? A gambler?"

Her father sighed. "So perhaps in Brand you picked a better man, after all."

"What you don't understand is that I love Brand. There is only Brand for me. Not Harry. Not anyone else. Ever."

"That cold bastard loves you." Her father paused, and Clea's heart gave a skip of surprise. "You should remind him that I am your father—and that if he turns me in, you will be devastated."

"Don't ask that of me," she begged. "Anything but that. Besides Brand would never compromise his beliefs. Not even for me."

Having the veil of innocence ripped from her eyes was excruciating…yet Clea knew the time had come to grow up. She was no longer Daddy's little girl, and she would not do this for him.

A wave of emotion swept across her father's face. At last only resignation remained. "That's that then. I'd better talk to my lawyer."

Clea closed the distance between them. "Oh, Daddy!"

Her father gave her a bear hug. "However this plays out, never forget that I love you. You're the best daughter a man could have."

Fourteen

Brand took one look at Clea's expression as she closed the front door behind her and resisted the demand to know where she'd been all this time. Instead, he scooped her into his arms and carried her into the study. Lowering himself into the chesterfield, he settled her on his lap and gazed into her ravaged eyes. "What happened?"

"You were right again—and now you're mopping up more tears. This is becoming a habit." Clea buried her face against his shirt front.

Pulling her closer into his embrace, he said, "I'd much rather be wrong every time if being right leaves you looking like you this." He was discovering that he had no stomach for being right when it brought her such pain.

"Oh, Brand!" She shuddered in his arms. "I went to see my father."

Brand stared over her head. If he'd known Clea was going to confront her father, he would've moved heaven and earth to make sure he was beside her. He didn't trust Donald Tomlinson with the most important person in his life—even if Clea was the man's daughter.

Resting his chin on top of her sweet-smelling hair, he decided that no man should have to face what he faced now. Going to the police to file charges against Donald Tomlinson could very well mean the end of him and Clea.

Brand was under no illusions. Doing the right thing was going to cost everything he'd lived for during the past four years...it was going to cost him his happiness. His wife. His child. *His family.*

Their marriage could not survive this disaster. Thinking about how his baby would grow up without its parents together made him contemplate the other option: He could keep quiet...and let Donald go free.

It was the most tempting decision of his life.

Yet Brand knew he couldn't be the man he considered himself to be if he allowed Donald—and Harry—to continue unchecked. Hadn't Clea told him that the reason she'd fallen in love with him had been because of his integrity?

Tightening his hold around Clea, he pressed his lips gently against her hair and told himself that at least he would have memories of having experienced a love many never discovered. It was cold comfort...but it would have to be enough.

"Sweetheart, you know I'm going to have to call the authorities, don't you?"

For long seconds Clea was silent.

Then she turned her head. Tears silvered her eyes. And Brand knew his heart was about to break.

"I'm so sorry, Brand, for doubting you. I thought you and D-Dad..." She stumbled over the word. "I thought it was just a personality clash, kind of like two strong-willed wolves. Pack leaders. I didn't see what was happening—how much he loathed you."

"I was a threat to him."

"That's what he said. Can you ever forgive me?"

The first fingers of hope touched him. Was it possible that Clea would stay, even if he turned her father in? But before he could reply, her face contorted.

Her hand went to her side. "Brand. The pain."

Panic filled him. "Where?"

She doubled over in his lap, not replying. Digging into his pocket, Brand searched for his cell phone. "Curtis? Has Smythe gone home?" He listened. "I need you to bring the Lincoln around. We're going to the hospital."

And then Brand started to pray.

The sound of the footfalls was heavier than those of the nurse who had just checked her blood pressure after helping Clea into the high, narrow hospital bed. Clea turned her head on the pillow as Brand entered the private ward.

His face was paler than Clea had ever seen it.

"How are you feeling?" he asked softly.

"A lot better now that I know the sharp pain in my sides was due to a ligament rather than something more serious." His concern warmed her. "And the baby's fine, too. There's no bleeding—thank heavens."

"But you need to rest—your blood pressure is higher than it should be, that's why they admitted you. Although, the medical team tell me it's already looking better."

Pulling up a chair, Brand dropped down beside her and covered his face with his hands. Clea touched his cheek. Immediately he glanced across at her, and the taut mask of worry softened.

"You *do* care," she whispered.

"Of course I care!"

"You've always been so difficult to read."

"We can't have that." He lowered his hands between his knees and sat forward on the edge of the chair. His lips curved up into the beginnings of a smile. "Look into my face, tell me what you see."

The translucence in his ocean eyes was blinding. Clea's breath caught at the unmasked emotion.

Was she seeing love for her there? Or was she seeing only his relief about the baby? Her heart started to pound. Clea was too scared to hope that the divide that had separated them had finally gone. *"Brand?"*

"I'm a man who lives by action, rather than words. Don't my actions tell you how I feel?" Propping his elbows on the edge of the bed, he leaned closer still. "I came back to you from hell."

That caused Clea to think about what was most causing her stress right now—the harm her father had done to Brand. Tentatively she asked, "Have you heard anything about my father?"

"Clea…" Brand rested a hand on hers. "The FBI are going to arrest him."

She shut her eyes. *So be it.* When she opened them again, Brand was still leaning forward, his eyes intent on her face.

"Clea, I'm going to be right beside you—whatever happens. Remember that. So try to let go of the worry."

"Thank you—I will."

What Brand was saying made sense. The baby—and Brand—were her priorities. Her father had made his own choices and he would have to bear the consequences for the harm, he'd caused Brand.

Forcing a smile, she said, "I will forever be grateful for the strength it took for you to come home to me."

"Then I had to put up with Harry hanging around, because you liked him, even when I wanted to take him out!"

Clea snorted. "Don't even remind me about how I let myself be taken in. But self-restraint is good for you—violence is never the answer...and that's what we're going to teach our child."

"No, love is," said Brand.

Clea's jaw dropped. "L-love?" she stuttered.

At that, his smile broke into a chuckle. "Oh, Clea! I might not be good with words, but I've already told you that it was only ever you. What more do you need me to say?"

Her eyes softening, Clea gazed at him. "That you love *me*?"

He gave her fingers a gentle squeeze. "Isn't it obvious?"

"Okay, maybe I have been dense," Clea admitted. "Forgive me?"

"Of course I forgive you, if you want to be forgiven. Oh, and don't forget I believed in our child without requiring scientific proof." His mouth quirked.

Clea started to smile. "That was definitely an act of love." Brand had always required scientific facts to accept anything; it had driven her mad in the past. "I should have realized that." Then her body jerked. "Ow!"

The laughter vanished, and he was on his feet. "Are you okay?"

"I'm fine and so is the baby." She took his hand and placed it on the rise of her belly. "The baby moved. Feel."

"Hey," Brand scolded the child in her stomach, "it's not your time yet. Stop kicking. Give your mother a break—she needs rest."

Actions, not words. Clea's lashes lowered as she drifted off to sleep. Although, when he chose to, he did words pretty well, too.

Actions, Clea reminded herself when she awakened in the morning to find Brand fast asleep beside her in the visitor's chair, his hand draped over hers, his long, lean length folded into the impossibly small space.

His eyes immediately peered as if he'd sensed her awakening, and he pulled his chair up closer to the bed. "How are you feeling, sweetheart?"

Clea turned her head on the pillow and smiled at him. "I'm ready to go home."

"The doctor came in earlier and said they're going to discharge you. Your blood pressure is back to normal. Everything is looking good...and the baby is fine," he said quickly as she started to sit up.

"So why do you still look worried?"

"Nothing to do with the baby, but a lot has happened over the past few hours."

"My father?"

Brand nodded.

"Tell me—I need to know." It brought great relief that Brand was treating her like an equal—he wasn't keeping secrets any longer.

"Harry surrendered to the FBI last night. He had some crazy idea that they might grant him immunity if he told them about your father."

A terrible sense of foreboding filled Clea. "Dad's not dead, is he?"

"No, but when the authorities arrived at his penthouse, he was gone."

"You're joking," Clea whispered, covering her mouth with her hands.

"I'm not." Brand held up three fingers. "Scout's honor. Apparently, it looked like the place had been ransacked. There were artifacts missing—small but exceedingly valuable pieces, according to what Harry told the Feds— and paintings had been cut from their frames. Your father's safe was open—his passport was nowhere to be found."

"Oh, my heavens!"

"He escaped."

"After I saw him last night, he knew you would go to the police. He'd finally run out of time." Clea discovered she wasn't surprised that her father had flown the coop—and taken a nest egg of treasures with him. No doubt he had a stash of money stored somewhere abroad as well. Going over their last conversation, she realized he'd already had it figured out—he'd told her he loved her, and that she was the best daughter a man could have. He'd been saying goodbye.

"He probably started setting up an escape hatch from the moment you arrived home," she said.

Brand nodded in agreement. "That's not all. Harry told the authorities that your father arranged for the death of a Baghdad taxi driver and poor Anita—and then had the bodies burned in my rental car to stage my death. So the charges are mounting. Of course, the FBI thinks Harry played a bigger role in this than he's admitting."

Clea shook her head. "I can't believe it. My best friend and my father. How will I ever be able to trust my judgment again?"

"You married me," Brand pointed out. "Nothing wrong with your judgment there."

"You're different—you've got integrity. Even my father recognized that."

Brand perched himself on the edge of her bed. "I'll admit that I'm torn. Your father is smart enough to head for a country that will have no extradition treaty with the United States. And, while I believe he should be jailed for what he did to me, and for the looting of priceless museum artifacts, I can't forget that he will always be your father."

Reaching up, Clea wrapped her arms around his neck, and kissed him. "I love you."

"I know," said Brand. "That's why you wanted the baby so badly."

Clea found herself smiling. "Actions not words."

"Exactly!" He bent his head and slanted his mouth across hers for a kiss that told her exactly how he felt about her.

One week later, Clea stopped dead in the doorway to her new—and much more spacious—office. She'd been appointed acting curator of the museum after Alan Daley had resigned over his involvement in purchasing the stolen artifacts for the museum. The final appointment still had to be made, but Clea had been left in no doubt that she would be awarded the position.

Brand was sitting in the chair behind her desk.

"What are you doing here?"

"Waiting for you. I was going to take you to dinner at Fives to celebrate." He glanced at the solitary clock on her office wall. It showed New York time. The other clock hadn't made the journey to this new space—Clea no longer needed it. "But we've missed the booking."

"Oh, I'm sorry. I slipped out to share tea with Mom." After the news had broken about her father, Clea had received an unexpected visit from her mother at the office. Now they were slowly reestablishing a relationship. Today, Clea had surprised herself by being gracious—and as she'd relaxed, she'd found herself actually liking her mother.

Warmed by the visible joy in her face. "What were we celebrating?"

"How about life?"

"What a good idea." Brand's nightmares had all but disappeared in the past week, as Clea cuddled up to him every night in their great big bed. "I'm sorry I wasn't here."

"No matter." He pushed the chair back from the desk and got to his feet, shrugging his jacket back on. "Are you hungry?"

"Starved," she admitted. "There are two of us to feed after all."

Sliding her an amused glance, Brand held out a hand. "Then let's go find something for you both to eat."

They settled on hot dogs from a stand on a street corner near Central Park.

It reminded Clea of those heady days when they'd first fallen in love, when their relationship had still been their secret joy, not yet revealed to the outside world.

"Let's walk through the park," she said impulsively.

They ate as they walked, and when she was done, Clea reached for Brand's hand and laced her fingers through his.

It was perhaps unsurprising that they ended up under the oak tree where Brand had first proposed. The golden rays slanting through the leaves gave the evening a magical glow. Brand turned her into his arms.

"I love you, Clea."

Her heart melted at the words.

"Will you marry me?"

Clea stared. "We're already married."

"I thought we might renew our vows. What do you say?"

Her answer came without hesitation. "Yes."

Brand groped in the pocket of his jacket before leaning

down to kiss her. When he straightened, he said, "Give me your hand."

So Brand had bought her another ring. A pang of regret pierced Clea. "I wish—" She broke off.

"What do you wish?"

She shook her head. "It's not important." This moment did not deserve to be tainted.

Metal slid along her finger, fitting perfectly. Clea glanced down.

She blinked in disbelief.

Three plaited strands of gold gleamed on her finger. "Brand!"

"I checked with museum security—"

"—they didn't have it." Clea completed his sentence. "I know, because that was the first place I asked. Where did you find it?"

"A Japanese woman turned it in at the police precinct closest to the museum." He grinned down at her. "Lucky I thought to check."

Clea remembered the curious faces of the tourists in the west wing gallery that day. "I will be forever indebted to her." She brushed her hand against the rise of her stomach. "It belongs to our family."

"Our family," he agreed, his arms settling around her shoulders. "You, me and the baby."

"Don't forget I want five boys," she breathed against his mouth, and Brand laughed softly. "They're going to have you wanting to disappear for another four years…"

"Never." He leaned against the solid trunk of the tree and drew her up against his chest. "I think those five sons will keep me too busy to go anywhere!"

Brand was home.

* * * * *

PASSION

For a spicier, decidedly hotter read—
this is your destination for romance!

COMING NEXT MONTH
AVAILABLE DECEMBER 6, 2011

#2125 THE TEMPORARY MRS. KING
Kings of California
Maureen Child

#2126 IN BED WITH THE OPPOSITION
Texas Cattleman's Club: The Showdown
Kathie DeNosky

#2127 THE COWBOY'S PRIDE
Billionaires and Babies
Charlene Sands

#2128 LESSONS IN SEDUCTION
Sandra Hyatt

#2129 AN INNOCENT IN PARADISE
Kate Carlisle

#2130 A MAN OF HIS WORD
Sarah M. Anderson

You can find more information on upcoming Harlequin® titles,
free excerpts and more at www.HarlequinInsideRomance.com.

HDCNM1111

REQUEST YOUR FREE BOOKS!
2 FREE NOVELS PLUS 2 FREE GIFTS!

Harlequin

Desire

ALWAYS POWERFUL, PASSIONATE AND PROVOCATIVE

YES! Please send me 2 FREE Harlequin Desire® novels and my 2 FREE gifts (gifts are worth about $10). After receiving them, if I don't wish to receive any more books, I can return the shipping statement marked "cancel." If I don't cancel, I will receive 6 brand-new novels every month and be billed just $4.30 per book in the U.S. or $4.99 per book in Canada. That's a saving of at least 14% off the cover price! It's quite a bargain! Shipping and handling is just 50¢ per book in the U.S. and 75¢ per book in Canada.* I understand that accepting the 2 free books and gifts places me under no obligation to buy anything. I can always return a shipment and cancel at any time. Even if I never buy another book, the two free books and gifts are mine to keep forever.

225/326 HDN FEF3

Name	(PLEASE PRINT)	
Address		Apt. #
City	State/Prov.	Zip/Postal Code

Signature (if under 18, a parent or guardian must sign)

Mail to the **Reader Service:**
IN U.S.A.: P.O. Box 1867, Buffalo, NY 14240-1867
IN CANADA: P.O. Box 609, Fort Erie, Ontario L2A 5X3

Not valid for current subscribers to Harlequin Desire books.

Want to try two free books from another line?
Call 1-800-873-8635 or visit www.ReaderService.com.

* Terms and prices subject to change without notice. Prices do not include applicable taxes. Sales tax applicable in N.Y. Canadian residents will be charged applicable taxes. Offer not valid in Quebec. This offer is limited to one order per household. All orders subject to credit approval. Credit or debit balances in a customer's account(s) may be offset by any other outstanding balance owed by or to the customer. Please allow 4 to 6 weeks for delivery. Offer available while quantities last.

Your Privacy—The Reader Service is committed to protecting your privacy. Our Privacy Policy is available online at www.ReaderService.com or upon request from the Reader Service.

We make a portion of our mailing list available to reputable third parties that offer products we believe may interest you. If you prefer that we not exchange your name with third parties, or if you wish to clarify or modify your communication preferences, please visit us at www.ReaderService.com/consumerchoice or write to us at Reader Service Preference Service, P.O. Box 9062, Buffalo, NY 14269. Include your complete name and address.

HDES11B

*Lucy Flemming and Ross Mitchell shared a magical,
sexy Christmas weekend together six years ago.
This Christmas, history may repeat itself when they find
themselves stranded in a major snowstorm...
and alone at last.*

*Read on for a sneak peek from
IT HAPPENED ONE CHRISTMAS
by Leslie Kelly.*

Available December 2011, only from Harlequin® Blaze™.

EYEING THE GRAY, THICK SKY through the expansive wall of windows, Lucy began to pack up her photography gear. The Christmas party was winding down, only a dozen or so people remaining on this floor, which had been transformed from cubicles and meeting rooms to a holiday funland. She smiled at those nearest to her, then, seeing the glances at her silly elf hat, she reached up to tug it off her head.

Before she could do it, however, she heard a voice. A deep, male voice—smooth and sexy, and so not Santa's.

"I appreciate you filling in on such short notice. I've heard you do a terrific job."

Lucy didn't turn around, letting her brain process what she was hearing. Her whole body had stiffened, the hairs on the back of her neck standing up, her skin tightening into tiny goose bumps. Because that voice sounded so familiar. *Impossibly* familiar.

It can't be.

"It sounds like the kids had a great time."

Unable to stop herself, Lucy began to turn around, wondering if her ears—and all her other senses—were deceiving her. After all, six years was a long time, the mind could play tricks. What were the odds that she'd bump into *him*, here? And today of all days. December 23.

Six years exactly. Was that really possible?

One look—and the accompanying frantic thudding of her heart—and she knew her ears and brain were working just fine. Because it was *him.*

"Oh, my God," he whispered, shocked, frozen, staring as thoroughly as she was. "Lucy?"

She nodded slowly, not taking her eyes off him, wondering why the years had made him even more attractive than ever. It didn't seem fair. Not when she'd spent the past six years thinking he must have started losing that thick, golden-brown hair, or added a spare tire to that trim, muscular form.

No.

The man was gorgeous. Truly, without-a-doubt, mouth-wateringly handsome, every bit as hot as he'd been the first time she'd laid eyes on him. She'd been twenty-two, he one year older.

They'd shared an amazing holiday season.

And had never seen one another again.

Until now.

Find out what happens in
IT HAPPENED ONE CHRISTMAS
by Leslie Kelly.
Available December 2011, only from Harlequin® Blaze™

Harlequin® *Desire*

ALWAYS POWERFUL, PASSIONATE AND PROVOCATIVE.

USA TODAY BESTSELLING AUTHOR

MAUREEN CHILD

BRINGS YOU THE CONCLUSION OF

KINGS *of* CALIFORNIA

THE TEMPORARY MRS. KING

Sean King vowed never to marry. But in order to win the land he needs to build an exclusive resort, he has to marry Melinda Stanford…and the Kings always win. Melinda agrees to a marriage in name only, but soon finds herself contemplating a true marriage to her compelling husband. But how can she love a man who agreed to leave her? And will he want to stay if she lays her heart on the line?

Available December wherever books are sold

n o c t u r n e™

NEW YORK TIMES AND USA TODAY
BESTSELLING AUTHOR

NALINI SINGH

brings you the exciting conclusion
to the four-book, multi-author miniseries

ROYAL HOUSE *of* SHADOWS

Micah is a feared monster, the dark Lord who condemns
souls to damnation in the Abyss. He has no idea he
is the last heir and only hope for Elden…only the
daughter of his enemy knows. Liliana is nothing like her
father, the Blood Sorcerer who cursed Micah. She sees
past Micah's armor and craves his sinful touch. Liliana
will have to brave his dangerous lair and help him
remember his past, or all hope for Elden will be lost.

LORD OF THE ABYSS
Also available as a 2-in-1 that includes
Desert Warrior.

Available in December wherever books are sold.

Harlequin®

ROMANTIC
SUSPENSE

USA TODAY BESTSELLING AUTHOR

MARIE FERRARELLA

Brings you another exciting installment from

CAVANAUGH
JUSTICE

A Cavanaugh Christmas

When Detective Kaitlyn Two Feathers follows a kidnapping case outside her jurisdiction, she enlists the aid of Detective Thomas Cavelli. Still reeling from the discovery that his father was a Cavanaugh, Thomas takes the case, thinking it will be a nice distraction...until Kaitlyn becomes his ultimate distraction. As the case heats up and time is running out, Thomas must prove to Kaitlyn that he is trustworthy and risk it all for the one thing they both never thought they'd find—love.

Available November 22 wherever books are sold!

www.Harlequin.com